DOCTOR·WHO

Sick Building

PAUL MAGRS

BBC
BOOKS

2 4 6 8 10 9 7 5 3 1

First published in 2007 by BBC Books, an imprint of Ebury Publishing.
A Random House Group Company. This paperback edition published in 2014.

Copyright © Paul Magrs, 2007

Doctor Who is a BBC Wales production for BBC One
Executive Producers: Russell T Davies and Julie Gardner
Series Producer: Phil Collinson

Original series broadcast on BBC Television. Format © BBC 1963.
'Doctor Who', 'TARDIS' and the Doctor Who logo are trademarks of the
British Broadcasting Corporation and are used under licence.

The Random House Group Ltd Reg. No. 954009.

Addresses for companies within the Random House Group can be found at:
www.randomhouse.co.uk.

A CIP catalogue record for this book is available from the British Library.

ISBN 978 1849909365

The Random House Group Limited supports the Forest Stewardship
Council® (FSC®), the leading international forest-certification organisation.
Our books carrying the FSC label are printed on FSC®-certified paper. FSC is
the only forest-certification scheme supported by the leading environmental
organisations, including Greenpeace. Our paper procurement policy can be
found at: www.randomhouse.co.uk/environment

Series Consultant: Justin Richards
Project Editor: Steve Tribe
Cover design by Lee Binding © BBC 2007

Typeset in Albertina and Deviant Strain
Printed and bound in Great Britain by Clays Ltd, St Ives PLC

For my brother, Mark

She was running through the winter woods because death was at her heels.

'It's on its way. It's coming!'

That was what she heard.

There were rumours on the air. Mutterings and whisperings in the woods. Danger approaching. Something bad. Creatures were abandoning the forest. Creatures she would usually make her prey. So her daily forages for food had sent her farther and farther afield. And even there, the story was the same. Where was everyone going? What was all the panic about?

'Get away,' they told her. Even creatures that should have been terrified of her. 'Get away from here, if you've got any sense. Get back to your den. Get back to your family. But even there you won't escape. There is no escape. Not from what's coming.'

7

She hadn't understood. What were they screeching about? What had caused this wave of terror in the winter woods?

She could smell it herself, though she could make no sense of it. The air reeked of danger. She knew something bad was coming. And so she had stopped hunting and fled for home. Now she was cut, bleeding and starving. Fallen branches cracked and splintered beneath her powerful limbs as she ran. She pounded through the undergrowth, sending up flurries of snow behind her.

She was a survivor. She had to get back. She had left her home for too long. It was vulnerable. To the elements, to outside attack. To the thing that was coming for them all. Her cubs were there. She hoped they were still there. She allowed herself to think of them briefly – three, hungry as she was, calling out for her in the musky gloom of their den. The thought made her redouble her efforts even though her muscles and sinews were cracking, almost at breaking point.

She had half-killed herself. Leaving this frozen forest that was her home, for the next valley. And what for? What had she learned there?

Nothing good.

It was the deepest part of winter. The air itself seemed stiff with ice. With each passing moment she could hear, even louder, the whispers and the hints that danger – and more than danger, certain death – was on its way. But she couldn't abandon her den. Her children were too young. If she tried to move them now, they would all surely die.

She had to be strong for all of them. But she was battered, bruised and bleeding. One of her long, curved teeth was snapped and splintered. Her savage claws were ragged and torn. Even so, all she could think about was her cubs. All she cared about was making them safe, any way she could.

Death was on its way.

And she was helpless in the face of that. 'Flee,' the smaller creatures warned her. 'Take your babies and run. Soon, there will be nothing here. Nothing can withstand what is on its way. We will all perish beneath that onslaught.'

'But… what is it?' she asked them.

None of them could describe it. None of them had a name for it. Something totally foreign. Something unutterably powerful and deadly.

So she ran. She turned tail to run home. She came howling through the winter woods, crashing through the densely packed trees. Wherever everyone else was fleeing to, she would join them. No matter where it led. Did they even know where there was safety? No one did. Maybe there was nowhere safe any more. But still she ran. Still she had to try. She had to find something to feed her children. And then they all had to leave home. They had to face the worst of the winter together.

They had to survive, and that was all there was to it.

She was almost home when something quite extraordinary happened.

She had reached a glade that she recognised. It was an open patch of frosted grass. There was a frozen stream and she was considering a pause to crack the ice and to slake her thirst. But before she could even slow down her hurtling pace, the frigid air was shattered by a loud and distressingly alien noise.

She flung down her powerful forepaws and thundered to a halt. Hackles up, she sniffed the disturbed air. Birds screeched and wheeled. Tortured, ancient engines were labouring away somewhere close. Was this it? Was this the approaching death that she had heard so much about? Had it found her already?

As the noise increased in pitch and intensity, and a solid blue shape began to materialise in the glade, the cat threw back her massive head and roared. Her savage jade eyes narrowed at the sight of the unknown object as it solidified before her, the light on its roof flashing busily.

Soon the noise died away. But there was a strange smell. Alien. And there were creatures within that blue box. She could almost taste their warmth and blood. And she remembered that she was starving.

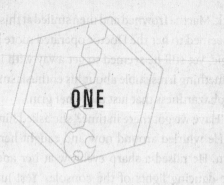

ONE

Martha Jones stood back as the Doctor whirled around the central control console of the TARDIS. She had only been travelling with him for a short time, but she knew that when his behaviour was as frenetic as it was now, the best thing was to stand back and wait until he calmed down.

She was a slim, rather beautiful young woman with a cool, appraising stare. She wore a tight-fitting T-shirt, slim-cut jeans and boots. The outfit was a practical one, she had found, for racketing about the universe in the Doctor's time-spacecraft.

The Doctor's activities seemed to be coming to an end, as the glowing central column on the console slid to a halt. The deafening hullabaloo of the engines suddenly faded away. The Doctor picked up a handy toffee hammer and gave the panel closest to him a hefty wallop, as if for luck. Martha frowned and then smiled at this. Sometimes it seemed to her the Doctor operated more by luck than logic, yet still he seemed to get away with it. There was something irresistible about his enthusiasm and general haphazardness that just made her grin.

'Have we got there in time?' she asked him.

He whirled around now and caught her laughing at him. He raised a sharp eyebrow at her and pointed to the dancing lights of the console. 'Yes! Just in time! I think.' He stopped. 'In time for what?' He ran his hands distractedly through his tangled dark hair.

'I don't know,' she said. 'You muttered something about saving somebody, or something. And getting there in time. Some awful kind of danger…'

'That's it!' he cried. 'I hadn't realised I'd told you so much about it already.' Now he was haring off round the console again.

'Hardly anything,' she protested. 'What kind of danger?'

His head popped up over the console and his expression was very serious, bathed in the green and satsuma orange glow of the TARDIS interior. 'The Voracious Craw,' he said, very solemnly.

'I see,' she said.

'Ooooh, they're a terrible lot,' he said, gabbling away twenty to the dozen. 'Each one is the size of a vast spaceship. They just go sailing about with their mouths hanging open, devouring things. Devouring everything they come across. They look just like, I dunno, gigantic inflated tapeworms or something. Only much worse. If your planet attracts a Voracious Craw into your orbit… well. I don't hold out much hope. No sirree. They just go… GLLOOMMPP! And that's the end of you. That's the end of everything. They're just so… voracious, you see.'

Martha gulped. 'My planet? They're heading for Earth?'

'What?' His eyes boggled at her. 'Are they?'

'You said…'

'Nononononono,' he yelled. 'I never said *your* planet. I said *a* planet, *any* planet. You really should stop being so… Earth-centric, Martha. I'm showing you the, whatsitcalled, cosmos here, you know.'

'Which world then?' she asked him, quite used to these rather infuriating lapses in his concentration.

A picture of a pale green, frozen world appeared on the scanner screen. 'This one,' said the Doctor, jamming his glasses onto his face. Every single facial muscle was contorted into an almighty frown as he gazed at the implacable planet. 'We're in orbit. Around somewhere called… ah yes. Tiermann's World. Named after its only settlers. Never heard of it.'

'And this Voracious thing is headed towards it?'

The Doctor stabbed a long finger at a grey blob that

Martha had taken to be a featureless land mass. 'There it is. Circling the world. Chomping its way through continents.'

'But it's huge!' she cried.

'And, according to the instruments, it's heading towards the only human settlement on that whole planet. They've got about thirty-six hours.' He whipped off his glasses, jammed them into the top pocket of his pinstriped suit and flashed her a grin. 'What do you reckon to whizzing down there and tipping them off, eh? They might not even know they're about to be gobbled up by a massive... flying tapeworm nasty space thingy.'

His hands were scurrying over the controls again, before she could even reply. The vworping brouhaha of the ship's engines drowned out any thoughts she might have aired at this point. Instead Martha peered at what she could see on the screen of the Voracious Craw, and imagined what it would look like from down on the surface. What it would be like to gaze up into the mouth of a creature that could eat whole worlds...

She was jerked out of her reverie by the Doctor tapping her briskly on her shoulder. 'C'mon. We've got vital stuff to do, you know. People to warn. Lives to save.' He paused and stared at the console for a moment. Martha wasn't sure if she was imagining it, but the constant burbling noise of the myriad instruments sounded somewhat different. 'Hmmm,' said the Doctor. 'She doesn't sound very happy. Too close to the Voracious Craw. It doesn't do to get too close to one of those. They can have some very strange and debilitating effects.'

'Oh, great,' said Martha.

'We'd best get on,' the Doctor said. 'The TARDIS will be OK. I hope.' He patted the controls consolingly, and then hurried out.

Martha followed him down the gantry to the white wooden doors of the TARDIS. She was bracing herself for what they were about to face out there, but at the same time she was exhilarated. Wherever they wound up, it was never, ever dull. Literally anything could happen, once they stepped through those narrow doors and into a new time and place.

The Doctor was striding ahead and she knew that his eagerness was not just about saving the human settlers. He was also quite keen on seeing this Voracious Craw about its terrible work. 'They're quite rare, these days, you know, our Voracious pals,' he said, grasping the door handle. 'Even I haven't seen an awful lot of the nasty things. Not properly close up, anyway.' He grinned jauntily and stepped outside onto the frozen grass of the glade. 'Ah,' he said.

Martha stepped past him. 'What is it?'

He nodded at the bulky form of the female sabre-toothed tiger before them. She was ready to spring. Her low-throated growl made the very air tremble. She was baring her fangs and one of them, Martha noticed absurdly, was broken. Her glittering green eyes pinned the time travellers to the spot and there was no malice nor enmity there. Just hunger.

'Whoops,' said the Doctor. 'Should've had at least a glance at the scanner before we stepped out. That was you,' he glanced at Martha. 'Distracting me with all your chat.'

She shushed him. He'd make the creature pounce, she just knew it. 'Do something!'

'Um,' he said. 'Right.' Then he stepped forward boldly. 'Good morning. I do hope we're not disturbing you, calling in unexpectedly like this…'

The sabre-tooth threw back her head and gave out the most blood-chilling cry that Martha had ever heard. There was real pain and desperation in that sound. It was savage and yet eloquent. And Martha knew, suddenly, that they were both going to die.

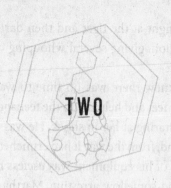

TWO

They were rescued by the blundering arrival of a young human male.

He was wearing heavy plastic coveralls against the weather, and he was loaded down with bagfuls of sophisticated camera equipment. He was so preoccupied with checking the display on one of these devices that he wandered straight into the space between the Doctor and Martha and the beast that was about to spring at them.

The teenager's head jerked up at the sound of the Doctor's voice. 'Get back!' he yelled, as the sabre-tooth pounced. Martha found herself darting forward and grabbing the boy by his fur-lined hood and wrenching him to one side, where they both landed, full length in the frosty grass. She whipped her head around to see what was happening to the Doctor. He had flung himself straight at the tiger and then darted off in the other direction, giving several whooping cries in order to distract it.

Martha knew there was no time to waste. She was back on her feet and helping up the teenage boy. He was dazed and staring at her in shock. He was clutching his knapsack and, from the way it had crunched underneath them, most of his equipment was useless now. His face was pale and somehow arresting. Martha followed his gaze and saw that the Doctor and the sabre-tooth had gone very still again. Near-silence had fallen in the glade. What had happened? For one heart-stopping second she had seen her friend fall under the vast, savage bulk of the forest creature. But now, seconds later, here he was, standing and staring earnestly into the tiger's eyes. The tiger was passive and mesmerised. The Doctor was speaking in a very low, persuasive voice.

He heard Martha step forward. 'Don't come any closer,' he warned her gently. 'She's calm, but anything could break her mood. She's hurt and frightened. Stay over there, Martha. We're just having a little chat…'

Martha and the boy exchanged a mute glance. So he could talk to the animals now, could he?

'See to your children,' the Doctor was saying. 'Do your best to get them to safety. You don't need to harm us. Look after yourself. Hurry. There isn't much time.'

The flanks of the great beast were heaving with

fury and anguish. But, as the Doctor spoke to her, she was calming. She growled, low in her throat and it was almost a purr.

'Go now,' the Doctor told her. 'We must all use the time wisely.'

The great cat turned on her heel and padded towards the trees once more. She spared them one more glance and Martha felt herself stiffen with fear. If that thing had decided it was going to kill them, they wouldn't have stood a chance. She held her breath until the cat had been swallowed up by the trees, and the crackling and snapping of frozen undergrowth had faded away.

The Doctor turned to his companions with a colossal 'Whewwww! Blimey!!' of relief. 'I'm glad that worked out. Could've been a bit messy otherwise.'

'It was a sabre-toothed tiger!' Martha gasped. 'On an alien planet?'

The Doctor gave a carefree shrug. 'They crop up everywhere. Maybe it's a world of prehistoric beasties. Dunno.' He fixed the teenage boy with a sharp stare. 'And you are?' Before the boy could reply, the Doctor shouted at him: 'You could have been killed, bursting in like that! Couldn't you see the danger? It was about twelve-foot long! Couldn't you watch where you were going?'

The boy was trembling with delayed shock, Martha could see. He brushed his long black hair out of his eyes and faced up to the Doctor's angry scrutiny. 'I... didn't see it. We don't come out here much. I'm… not… used to it out… h-here.' Suddenly he looked much younger and very, very scared. Martha judged that he couldn't have been much more than fifteen. He was looking around the wintry glade with sheer terror and confusion. Martha was secretly pleased that she was dealing with being in this place so much better than this apparent native. Here she was on an alien world and – besides the sabre-tooth encounter – she was cool as anything.

The Doctor's voice dropped and became kinder. 'What's your name, and who are you?'

'Solin, sir—'

'Doctor. And this is my friend, Martha. We're here to help you.'

'Help me?'

The Doctor nodded firmly. 'You, your people. The human settlement here.'

'My family,' the boy said. 'We are the only people here. Under the dome. In Dreamhome. There are only three of us.'

'Three!' the Doctor smiled. 'Well, that should make things a bit easier.'

Solin's face was creased with puzzlement. 'But I don't understand… Why would we need your help? We have everything we need in Dreamhome. Everything we will ever need. That's what Father says.'

'Hmm, he does, does he?' smiled the Doctor. 'Well,

you saw what that sabre-tooth was like. She's got wind of something. Something really, really bad is on its way.' The Doctor did his heavy-frown thing, Martha noticed, when his eyebrows jumped and set themselves at a very serious angle. 'You lot really need my help. And Martha's. Martha's help is indispensable, too.'

'We already know something bad is coming,' muttered the boy. He looked sullen.

'What's all this stuff?' Martha was picking up pieces of futuristic equipment that had flown out of Solin's knapsack. Solin took them from her, sighing at the damage. 'I was taking pictures. That's why I'm out here, in the forest. Normally I wouldn't, but I thought… this is the last time, my last chance. And Father said he could send out the Staff and they would take all the pictures I wanted, of whatever I wanted. But it isn't the same, is it?'

'No,' said Martha, though she couldn't make head nor tail of what he was on about.

'Why was it your last chance?' asked the Doctor, testing him out.

Solin was tying up his bag and hoisting it onto his back. 'Because my father says that we have to leave this world. We have to get aboard the ship that brought us here and go somewhere else. He has sensed the danger, too, Doctor. Same as that sabre-tooth did. He knows we have to leave here. We're already going, Doctor.'

* * *

It took them some time to get through the woods onto the track that Solin assured them would lead to Dreamhome. As they went, ducking under branches and shimmying past trunks, the air was growing colder. The sky was closing in and darkening so they could see less and less of their new environment. There was something eerily quiet about the forest. To Martha, it seemed as if the whole place and all the remaining life forms in it were holding their breath. There was a curious atmosphere, of the whole place waiting for something dreadful to happen.

'So you've lived here all your life?' she called ahead to Solin, hoping that their voices would dissipate this feeling of anxiety.

'I was born on the ship before we landed here,' he replied. 'I've never known anywhere else. This is my home.'

To Martha's eyes, he seemed unaccustomed to being in the forest. He tripped and swore a couple of times as he led them through the undergrowth, and he seemed, at times, unsure of the direction to take. The Doctor was studying him carefully, Martha noticed, just as he studied the strange plant life, all petrified by frost as they made their gradual progress.

'I've lived in Dreamhome all my life,' Solin admitted. 'Father says there isn't much point in our going outside. All of this...' he gestured at the twilit woods about them.

'We can watch all of this on our screens. We can send out the staff for anything we might need from here. My father says it's all much better for us, and safer, under the dome.'

'I'm sure it is,' said the Doctor thoughtfully. 'But what about having a sense of adventure, eh? What about exploring places for yourself?'

Solin looked piqued. 'Well, I'm out here, aren't I? I've disobeyed Father.'

'Quite,' grinned the Doctor. 'Well done.' Martha could see that the Doctor wasn't that impressed by Solin's sense of adventure. But why would he be, Martha wondered. The Doctor wandered about at will through all time and space, insatiably curious and amazed by everything he saw and experienced. He was never afraid of what he might come up against, and he didn't see why anyone else should be fearful, either.

'You're settlers from Earth, then?' the Doctor asked. 'A scientific expedition?'

Solin shook his head. 'My father was a scientist once. But he retired here. He bought this world, many years ago.'

'Bought?' said the Doctor. 'He must be rolling in it, your dad.'

'He was an inventor, back on Earth. He made a lot of money in the Servo-furnishing industry.'

'The what?' Martha asked. But the Doctor shushed

her. They had stopped at a gap in the trees. Ahead of them, in the frozen gloaming, the forest simply stopped. A shimmering force field blocked their way. And beyond it lay fresh spring grass, starred with daisies. A perfect lawn stretched several hundred yards ahead of them, running up to a series of verdant box hedges, which fitted neatly around what appeared to be a pale yellow mansion house.

'Wow,' Martha sighed. 'That's your Dreamhome, is it?'

Solin looked relieved to be within sight of the building. 'That's right. We made it here at last.' He glanced at the dark forest at their backs. 'We're late. Father will be furious.'

'Won't he be alarmed, that we've come visiting?' asked the Doctor.

'It's true, we've hardly ever had visitors here,' Solin said, moving towards the rippling air of the force field. 'A couple of old cronies of Father's. But mostly he's turned his back on the rest of the universe. I imagine it will be a pleasant surprise indeed, that you're here.'

'I hope he's friendly,' said the Doctor, pulling a face. He was carefully watching what Solin did, as the teenager approached what appeared to be an old-fashioned red pillar box in the middle of the forest clearing. He swung open a panel on the front and jabbed at the buttons inside. Frustratingly, neither the Doctor nor Martha could see exactly which buttons he pressed. Immediately, a gap opened up in the transparent shield.

'Quickly,' Solin told them. 'The door only opens for twenty seconds at a time. It's a security thing. And the shields have been a bit unreliable the past couple of days. We must go in right now.'

The Doctor grinned. 'After you, Martha,' he said, and bent to have a good look at the red pillar box. 'I like the style of it. Techno gizmos and whatsits disguised as old Earth tat. Very stylish. I'm looking forward to meeting your father, Solin.'

Solin looked back at the Doctor and his face was glum and dark. *Hmm*, thought Martha, as she eased ahead and slipped through the door in the force shield. *There's something funny going on, definitely. That boy has got issues, I reckon.*

But, in the meantime, Martha was bowled over by what she discovered on the other side of the doorway. As soon as she passed through the shimmering, hissing shield, she found that the temperature was suddenly like a balmy midsummer evening. The sky above was clear and glinting with alien stars. The lawn beneath her feet rippled gently with luscious grass. She stamped the thick, clodded snow off her boots and sighed deeply. 'I think I'm going to like Dreamhome, Solin,' she said.

The Doctor stepped up behind her, gazing appreciatively at their new trappings. 'I wouldn't get too used to it,' he murmured in her ear. 'Remember. The Voracious Craw's on its way. This place's days are numbered. Its hours are numbered. Its very minutes are ticking away…'

'But this place is shielded…' Martha said. 'Surely the Craw thing can't gobble its way through… Can it?'

'Oooh, yes,' nodded the Doctor. 'And that's why we're here. To make sure they are sufficiently alarmed.'

As if on cue, a vile wailing noise erupted from the pillar box on the other side of the gap in the force shield. Martha and the Doctor covered their ears and whirled about to see Solin panicking at the controls.

'What is it?' the Doctor dashed over, brandishing his sonic screwdriver. He was like a gunslinger, Martha thought, the way that thing flew out of his pocket and into his hand.

'It's broken!' Solin wailed, above the ghastly fracas. 'Somehow… I've gone and broken the shields! Great holes are opening up all over the Dreamhome!'

The Doctor angled in to have a go with his sonic. 'Never mind. I bet it's the Craw affecting the circuitry. It's bound to be. It sets up this great wave of interference before it strikes. Let me see. I'll just have a…'

'No, Doctor, you don't understand,' Solin cried. 'The defences are down! They've never malfunctioned like this before! Dreamhome is vulnerable to outside attack now! And it's all my fault! I've ruined everything!'

THREE

This was precisely the kind of thing the Doctor loved. 'Let me have a go,' he said, 'I'm sure I can get it working again. In a flash, I bet you! I'll just give it a good sonicking…'

Martha rolled her eyes, and saw that the boy's agitation was way out of proportion. He looked appalled at himself suddenly. 'I should never have gone out into the woods,' he said. 'Father is so right. I could have been killed…'

'Hmmm,' said the Doctor, not really listening. His head was jammed inside the pillar box as he examined the workings of the force shields. 'It all seems very straightforward to me – ooowwwwwww.' A shower of sparks sent him spinning backwards. He sucked his burnt fingers ruefully.

'We aren't supposed to tamper with the workings of Dreamhome,' Solin said, in a doleful voice. 'We are supposed to leave it all to the Servo-furnishings.'

The Doctor was about to ask him what he was going on about, when Martha said: 'And these Servo-furnishings… Would they happen to be the things heading across the lawn towards us?'

'Oh,' said the Doctor, taken aback. 'Wow. They look just like…'

'Oh no,' said Solin, pitifully, as if he'd been caught out doing something really bad.

Martha said, 'They look just like a lawnmower and a water cooler. Why are they speeding towards us like that?'

'D'you know, she's right?' laughed the Doctor delightedly, as they watched the machines come ambling at speed across the manicured grass towards them. 'That's brilliant! I love them! Look at them go!'

'I'm in for it now,' Solin sighed.

Martha was quite correct. Dreamhome – or rather, the infinitely complex and advanced living computer at Dreamhome's heart – had despatched the two Servo-furnishing robots that had been closest to the breach in the force shield. The lawnmower and the water cooler had both immediately ceased what they were doing by the tennis courts and now they were hastening towards the scene of the incident. They bustled self-importantly up to the pillar box at the edge of the lawn, utterly ignoring the humanoids that stood there.

'They're fantastic, Solin! Proper robots! Proper futuristic robots!' The Doctor examined the Servo-furnishings as they busied themselves at the pillar box controls, flexing precision tools and soldering wires like mad.

'Like something out of the 1950s,' Martha said. 'Like what people always thought the future was going to look like.'

'You're right,' grinned the Doctor. 'It's all a bit *Lost-in-Space*-y, isn't it?'

One of the robots turned its head and seemed to look the Doctor up and down. With a certain amount of scathing sarcasm, the Doctor thought, glaring back at the electronic brain in its see-through head. 'Tell me, Solin. Is everything in your house a robot?'

'Nearly everything,' Solin said. 'That's what my father made his fortune from. He designed and built the Servo-furnishings. So humanity would never have to dirty their hands with menial tasks, ever again.'

'Oh, really? Oh dear,' the Doctor frowned. 'There's nothing wrong with getting your hands dirty once in a while. Machines like this can make life a bit too easy, you know…'

Martha nudged him gently. 'I think Solin agrees with you. That's why he was out in the woods, taking pictures for himself, wasn't it?'

'Aha,' said the Doctor. 'And what—'

But he was interrupted by a booming voice that came calling across the lawn. It was a very cultivated voice and its richly rounded vowels made Solin flinch, Martha noticed. 'What is going on? Solin? What have you done? And who... who are these people?' The voice lost some of its grandness towards the end, as its owner spied the Doctor and Martha waving hello.

'Just keep on waving,' the Doctor hissed through gritted teeth. 'I'll do the explaining. And I'll say I damaged the force shield if you like, Solin.'

The large windows of the wing of Dreamhome closest to them had shot up and a very tall and dignified figure was stepping out into the evening air. He had a mane of silvery hair and a very neatly trimmed beard. He wore silver-purple robes which again, Martha thought, looked very space age and futuristic to her. He was also wearing a deep purple cloak, which billowed out around him as he strode crossly towards the newcomers.

'What have you done? You have endangered us all!'

'Good, um, evening,' called the Doctor. 'I think everything's under control now. I'm the Doctor and this is Martha and this is Solin and...'

'I know who Solin is,' said the tall figure coldly. 'He's my son. I am Professor Ernest Tiermann. I own this world.'

'You own the world, eh?' grinned the Doctor. 'That's impressive. What kind of council tax do you pay on that, eh? A whole world! Imagine, Martha. I bet the heating bills are outrageous. And by the way, did you know that the whole place is in the most horrible danger?'

Ernest Tiermann gazed down at the Doctor with cool, grey eyes. 'What concern is that of yours… Doctor?'

'I'm here to help!' smiled the Doctor. 'I came here because we detected humans. But there's all sorts of life forms here. Sabre-tooths! We met a scared female out in the woods. We need to think about rescuing as many life forms as we can, really. Before the whatsit arrives. The end of everything.'

Tiermann was watching the Servo-furnishings finish up repairing the force field. With an almighty crackle of energy the shield came down once more, sealing them all inside the dome which shimmered over the Dreamhome. Martha and the Doctor both heard Tiermann and his son give an audible sigh of relief. Now that the outside was firmly shut out, it seemed they could relax.

'Don't like the old outside much, do we?' said the Doctor.

'You'd better come into the house,' Tiermann snapped. 'Solin. You will be punished for your misadventures. Come along, all of you.'

With that, Tiermann turned on his heel and led them towards the imposingly beautiful homestead, where he and his family had lived for as long as Solin had been alive.

'Not much fun, your dad,' Martha whispered, as they hurried across the lawn.

'He's got a lot on his mind,' Solin told her. 'And you know, leaving this place is going to break his heart.'

As they were given their first glimpse of the interior of Dreamhome, Martha was beginning to understand why it would be such a difficult place to leave. It was the most luxurious and impressive home she had ever seen. The lustrous waxed wooden floors were so perfect and sheer it seemed a shame to stand on them. The walls were a glossy mahogany and the massive plate-glass windows were hung with the richest, most voluptuous curtains. And yet, for all the glamour and glitz of the furniture and fittings, there was nothing vulgar or overly ornate about the Dreamhome. It was all decorated with discreet good taste.

All of it was immaculate, too. As they progressed from hallway to reception room and into a vast drawing room, Martha and the Doctor were aware of Servo-furnishings of all sizes and functions hovering around them: dusting, polishing and tidying as they went. In the drawing room where Tiermann curtly bid them sit and make themselves comfortable, there was even a teak drinks cabinet that set about pouring them a sweet sherry each.

'Thanks,' Martha told the drinks cabinet uncertainly,

taking her drink.

The Doctor waved his away. 'Never touch the stuff, hardly. Well, I do admire all this, Tiermann. Very, very nice. Must have cost you a packet, this place.'

'Everything was imported from Earth,' Tiermann pronounced, with a faint sneer. 'All the woods and marble, the stone and the metals. Everything needed to build the Dreamhome. It was my dream that brought this place alive. And we thought that we would be here for ever.'

'Oh dear, never mind,' said the Doctor – rather glibly, Martha thought. 'Funny how things don't work out sometimes, isn't it?' He took the sherry glass out of Martha's hands with one easy movement and sniffed the drink sharply. 'You wouldn't like it. Bit too sweet.'

'Solin, go and tell your mother,' Tiermann addressed his son, who had been standing uneasily to one side, feeling responsible for the presence of these two strangers in the Dreamhome. 'Would you fetch her and tell her that we have the most delightful, unexpected company?'

Solin nodded and hurried off fretfully.

The drinks cabinet swung round to offer Tiermann his own drink. Tiermann took it absent-mindedly, with the air – Martha thought – of one quite used to being waited on hand and foot by robotic servants every day of his life. He was grinning at his guests now but his expression still wasn't a very friendly one.

'We are grateful that you would come here to give us warning of the advancing danger, Doctor, Miss Jones,' he said graciously.

'All in a day's work,' said the Doctor, draining Martha's sherry glass with a large gulp. 'I'd be interested to hear what your plans are. You've been here a long time. The world beyond this one has changed quite a lot, I imagine.'

Tiermann grimaced. 'There should still be a place in it for Ernest Tiermann, Doctor. I was famed, you know. Right across this sector. For my inventions. My toys.'

'Rather valuable toys,' noted the Doctor. 'Robotic servants like these. They can be made to do anything. You could raise a whole army of them. That could be worth a lot to some people.'

Tiermann pulled a face. 'Mere toys. They could never hurt anyone, Doctor. That's not what the Servo-furnishings are for. Look at Walter, here. The drinks cabinet. His sole function is to supply us with our favourite tipple at the appropriate moment.'

'And I am very happy in my work,' said Walter, in a rather fruity mechanical voice. He was right behind Martha at the time, and she jumped. The Doctor laughed and held out his purloined glass for a refill.

'And they'll all be going with you, when you leave, I imagine?' He smiled at Walter and then at Tiermann. 'I imagine it'd be hard to leave your servants behind, eh?

I mean, after all this time, you must have got quite fond of them, eh?'

Tiermann's face had gone dark. 'They are simply machines, Doctor. It is pure foolishness to get attached to them. Machines run down and need replacing eventually. Quicker even than human beings do. My wife has fond, foolish ideas about the Servo-furnishings. And so does my son. But they are nothing really. Mechanical toys, that's all.'

'Hmmm,' said the Doctor. 'That seems a bit cold-hearted to me.' He reached over to pat the wooden head of the drinks cabinet called Walter. The head jerked abruptly and the Doctor snatched back his hand. 'There, there, Walter. I'm sure he didn't mean it. You're real to Martha and me, isn't he, Martha?'

Martha stared at the wooden robot and smiled uncertainly. 'Of course he is.'

But Walter turned and plodded away to his place by the wall, the bottles stowed in his interior clinking dully as he went.

'I'll never understand that ridiculous, sentimental impulse,' Tiermann sighed. 'To suppose that everything has feelings. Ha! Only we have feelings, Doctor. Only us. The human race.'

The Doctor slurped his sherry, grimacing at its sweetness. 'Don't be too sure of that, Professor Tiermann. That's a very narrow, heartless philosophy.'

Tiermann shrugged carelessly. 'We could debate that point for a very long time, Doctor. But we have only a very few hours – a little more than a day – before we have to leave. Philosophy must be put aside.'

'And compassion?'

'I leave such tender feelings to my wife and my son,' Tiermann said.

The Doctor and Martha were inspecting their allotted quarters. Even though they had protested that they weren't really going to be here for very long, Tiermann had insisted on taking them into two gorgeously appointed rooms with a connecting door. Tiermann was adamant that they stay and prepare themselves for dinner. Martha was glad to put her feet up after their traipse through the woods, but the Doctor kept interrupting her.

Three times he had rapped on the middle door and come marching in, saying: 'And another thing...' as he aired his many and varied thoughts on their visit so far, and vented his observations about their host. 'What did you think of him, eh? Bit chilly? Bit creepy?'

Martha had experience of surgeons and doctors, and some of them had struck her as just as heartless and dispassionate as Ernest Tiermann seemed to be. To them, their human patients were simply problems to solve. Their bodies were intricate machines that needed examining and possibly fixing. Rarely did these particular doctors think about the everyday lives or the feelings of the people whose ailments they considered. Perhaps, Martha thought, it would be distracting, or too upsetting, to think of them as real people. Perhaps that was how the medics protected their own emotions.

But Tiermann… About him she wasn't so sure.

Meanwhile she wanted to luxuriate and relax and think it all over. She had already discovered that her en suite bathroom contained a large claw-footed iron tub painted pale blue. She smiled at the Doctor, ushered him out, and told him to come back in at least half an hour.

'And another thing… he's so complacent,' the Doctor burst out. 'There's less than one and a half Earth days until this whole valley goes ker-splat, and what's old man Tiermann doing? He's inviting us to dinner! He's telling us to get all dressed up and how much his wife is looking forward to meeting us…'

The Doctor was exasperated, stomping up and down on the thick pile of the carpet in Martha's room. She had only just finished dressing, and the two robots that had been quietly helping her were standing back discreetly, to admire their handiwork. Martha was a vision in a pale cream gown, one run up for her especially by the robotic seamstress that had swept in, forty minutes ago, and taken her measurements in the wink of an eye. Now Martha was admiring her own reflection in a tall burnished mirror and eventually the Doctor's rant petered out and he stared at her.

'You look very nice,' he said. 'Why am I still in my same old suit? Where's my new threads?'

Martha shrugged bare shoulders. 'You've been too busy stomping up and down complaining about everything.'

The Doctor threw himself down on a silken divan and pulled at his hair distractedly. 'I've been checking this place out. It's outrageous, Martha. These people don't seem to do a single thing for themselves. These rooms are full of... pampering and preening machines...'

'I know,' she smiled, as one of the robots leaned in to help with her earrings. They were so quiet and skilful, it was almost like they weren't even there. It had only been an hour or so since she had entered Dreamhome, but already Martha was getting used to the easy luxury of the place. The bath she had slipped into had poured itself, adding just the right amount of bubbles and lotion. It had startled her only once, as she lay back, by speaking to her directly and asking if she wanted the hot water topping up. Apart from the occasional surprise like that, she could see herself getting quite accustomed to the automated facilities here.

The Doctor wasn't half so impressed. 'Mechanical chicanery! Cheap and nasty gee-gaws! That's all they are. Tiermann's no genius. He's just showing off with his tacky robots.'

One of Martha's helpers swung her slim fibre-glass body round and seemed to give the Doctor a nasty stare. Then she and her companion turned and swept out of the bedroom, apparently in high dudgeon.

'Now you've upset them,' said Martha. Her whole body was tingling with sheer luxurious delight. She felt as if she had indeed been pampered from top to toe and, what was more, she was looking forward to a civilised dinner.

'I'm just a bit wound up,' he sighed.

'By Tiermann?'

'I hate people putting on airs like that,' the Doctor said. 'I don't like his pomposity and his hubris and his… cockiness. Even when he knows everything here in this valley… the Dreamhome, the woods and everything, it's all going to be sucked up and stripped away, right into the waiting maw of the Voracious Craw. Hey, that rhymes.'

'He's a strange one, all right,' Martha said. 'But I think, underneath all the showing off, he's pretty conflicted.'

'I should cocoa,' said the Doctor, coming to examine his own tousled reflection in the mirror.

'It'll be hard for him, leaving here,' said Martha. 'Supposedly he's put his whole life into creating this environment. Surely he won't give all that up, without a fight?'

'Oh, there's no fighting when it comes to the Voracious Craw,' the Doctor told her. 'It's a case of run away very quickly indeed, or be sucked up into the sky with everything else animal, vegetable and mineral, and be turned into the biggest and nastiest smoothie in the world. Tiermann's not daft. He knows he has to go. We all have to go.'

The Doctor grinned at her and turned to lead the way out of their sumptuous suite of rooms. His words had sent a chill through Martha, however, as he brought home the danger that they were all in, just by staying here till the last moment. She thought that the Doctor was putting them both at risk, just as Tiermann was his family. The TARDIS was still back there, somewhere, in the dark heart of the frozen wilderness. Shouldn't they be setting about retrieving it?

But Martha took a deep, calming breath and decided that the Doctor probably knew best. She tested out walking in her new, exquisite shoes, and turned to follow her friend in to dinner.

FOUR

Tiermann's wife was called Amanda, and the first impression that the Doctor and Martha had of her was that she was very beautiful, but very quiet and demure.

'Small wonder,' the Doctor whispered, 'the way her old man keeps rabbiting on.'

Martha shushed him, as the canapé robot slid by, delectable nibbles arranged on his flattened head.

But it was quite true about Tiermann. He kept pacing up and down, spouting off about the wonders of the Dreamhome and his ubiquitous Servo-furnishings. As he stood by the fireplace, holding forth about everything he had invented, Martha could sense the Doctor's hackles rising as his irritation mounted.

Now Tiermann was bragging about the ship that had brought them to this world, and that would bear them safely away. 'I designed it myself, so many years ago. And its design still has never been surpassed. Here we are a few parsecs from Station Antelope Slash Nitelite, and that is where we will make our way to. They'll be very glad to see us and our miraculous craft, I am sure.'

Amanda Tiermann sat in a high-necked dress with flowing sleeves, cradling a tall glass filled to the brim with a foaming blue concoction. She smiled gently at Tiermann's braggardly statements and occasional jokes, but she volunteered few comments of her own. On being introduced to the Doctor and Martha she had simply said that she was delighted, and that they had had very few guests at Dreamhome over the years. Her eyes were a brilliant emerald, Martha noted, and there was a glint in them of... what? She wondered. Apology? Fear? Pleading? Something, at any rate, that Amanda could not express in front of her swaggering husband.

Solin, too, was quiet this evening. He was in a dark green suit and he seemed wary and watchful of his father.

'I'm just not convinced that you've made adequate plans for your escape, y'know,' said the Doctor airily. Martha saw Solin flinch at the way the Doctor interrupted his father's flow.

'Oh, really, Doctor?' purred Tiermann. He waved the canapé robot away from him crossly.

'Leaving it till the last minute. And, from what I've seen, you lot haven't done any packing yet or anything. I know some worlds, when they've had wind of the Craw on the way, they've upped and fled with weeks to spare.'

Tiermann shrugged. 'I don't like unnecessary panic. And there is no need for panic, Doctor.' He was growing agitated. 'It was this kind of niggling that I became a recluse to avoid… I got out of the rat race in order to prevent contact with…'

'People like me?' grinned the Doctor.

'People who get worked up. Who never sit long enough in one place to really think about things… about their place in this world…'

'You're a cool customer, Tiermann,' said the Doctor. 'I'll give you that.'

Tiermann took it as a compliment. Then his wife startled them all by speaking up: 'Ernest likes everything to be very civilised. He would hate to make an undignified exit from this planet which has been our home for so long.'

The Doctor studied her pale, perfect face. 'Well, yes. I can imagine. And it'll be a wrench, won't it? Zooming off to some manky old space port. Finding digs on Antelope Slash Nitelite for a bit. You're gonna be out of pocket when the Craw gobbles this place up, aren't you?'

'We'll hardly be paupers, Doctor,' Tiermann snapped.

Then a tall, butler-like robot came to the drawing room door, and bid them all come through for dinner.

Martha was hardly aware of what they ate, as the

courses came and went in the tense dining room. She sipped carefully at a pale orange soup, and picked at a delicate fish in creamy sauce and she could hardly taste a thing. She was on tenterhooks, knowing that some almighty row was brewing between the Doctor and Tiermann. She could feel it crackling on the air: palpable as the approach of the deadly Craw itself.

The Doctor almost seemed to be baiting their host. 'Ah, you can have too much luxury and ease, is the way I see it,' he was saying, sitting back in his chair. 'You lot, here, with all your gizmos and gadgets and servants doing everything, well, you don't really have to struggle or try to do anything for yourselves, do you? You can't have any zest or energy or relish in anything, can you?'

Tiermann glared back at him. His wife looked uneasy. There was a faceless robot sitting right next to Amanda and everyone had been too polite to draw attention to it. But Martha thought it was downright weird that, whenever Amanda leaned forward to take a mouthful of food or a drink or something, the robot next to her nipped in first and consumed it for her. Amanda didn't seem to mind at all. She behaved as if this was perfectly normal.

'You, Doctor, don't know what you're talking about,' Tiermann said. 'I think perhaps you envy us our lives here in the Dreamhome. Perhaps you've never known luxury and peace of mind.'

'Ha!' cried the Doctor. 'I've known enough to know that the former certainly doesn't lead to the latter. I think you're just burying your heads in the sand here. That's what you've been doing all these years. Hiding from the cosmos. Hoping it'll go away. Here in your perfectly tasteful paradise.'

'There's nothing wrong with good taste,' Tiermann said.

'But everything's so bland!' the Doctor burst out. 'This place is so tasteful, it's painful! Everything's beige and cream! There's nothing out of place! Everything's trying so hard to be inoffensive and easy on the eye! Even the food we're eating… It's tasteless! Boring!' He shoved his plate away with a clatter and there was an embarrassed pause. 'Um,' said the Doctor. 'That was a bit impolite, I suppose.'

Amanda smiled at him. 'Never mind, Doctor…'

Tiermann interrupted then, taking great offence at the Doctor's words. 'You can say what you want about my aesthetic tastes, Doctor. That's hardly going to hurt my feelings. But it does hurt me that you think I would gamble with the safety of my family.'

As their discussion went on and became ever more heated, Solin motioned to Martha. He whispered that maybe there was time, before dessert, to pop out onto the veranda for some cool air.

Outside there was a slight, ruffly breeze. Martha was

amazed that there could be any such thing, under the crackling force-shield dome that covered Dreamhome. But the stars were out and the air was cool, and the whole place gave the illusion that it was a gorgeous, perfect summer night. Even though she knew that, just beyond those trees, a hellish midwinter reigned supreme.

She sipped at her drink and smiled at Solin as he joined her, sitting on the concrete balcony.

'My father gets quite upset if he feels our way of life is being criticised.'

'The Doctor knows how to push people's buttons,' Martha admitted.

'And Father is touchy, too, because all this is coming to an end. He has to face the busy universe again. He dreads it. He feels like the Dreamhome experiment has failed, in a way.'

A slim robot slid out onto the veranda to stand by them. It held out a packet of cigarettes and, before Martha could protest that she never smoked, the machine had lit two and started smoking both.

'They really do everything for you, don't they?'

Solin grinned. 'It's a filthy habit.'

'I know that,' said Martha. 'But your poor mother. Does she never eat anything?'

'Hardly,' he said. 'And only when she's alone. Mother is very shy.'

'What about you, Solin?' Martha asked. She watched

him get up and wander away. He looked very pale and almost sickly in the stark moonlight. 'Haven't you been very lonely, growing up here with no one else your own age?'

'No,' he said. 'But then, I don't know what I'm missing, do I?'

'I suppose not,' she said. 'But have you really never met any other people besides your parents?'

'Oh, one or two. Father has had a handful of visitors over the years. No children, though. But… I've always had the staff to speak to, if I wanted other company. The Servo-furnishings are amazing. Just like real people, some of them, I imagine. They can be very lifelike. Even spontaneous.'

'Hmm,' Martha said, unconvinced. She eyed the robot next to them as it stubbed out both cigarettes and slid away, leaving a cloud of blue smoke. 'I don't think they're very like real people, to be honest. It's not like having brothers and sisters.'

'Do you have siblings, Martha?' Solin asked, sitting by her again.

'Oh yes,' she laughed. 'A whole bunch of them. Well, a brother and a sister. Just about drove me mental. But I'd never be without them. I couldn't imagine growing up without them.'

There came a much chillier breeze shushing past them and Martha shivered.

'Please, don't feel sorry for me,' Solin said. 'I've had everything I ever wanted, up till now.'

'All right,' Martha said. 'It's a pact. I won't feel sorry for you.'

'I like you, Martha Jones,' Solin said, rather abruptly. 'I think I am not only attracted to you, but I find that you are good company, too.'

'What?' Martha said. 'You can't just come out with stuff like that.'

He frowned. 'Why not?'

'Because it's... well, it's a bit embarrassing.'

He looked earnestly at her and she knew she was hurting his feelings. 'But I am attracted to you, Martha. I felt it straight away. And you are a nice person, too. I do like you. I want to tell you this.'

'Oh god,' Martha sighed. 'Social skills not high on the Dreamhome priority list, eh?'

'On the contrary,' Solin said, 'My manners, I hope, are impeccable. I hope I was very polite when I told you that I wanted to kiss you, and so on.'

'What?!' Martha started laughing at this. She couldn't stop for a few minutes. 'You're just a kid! Shut up! Stop saying that!'

'But I...' Solin stopped. Martha looked up to see fury flooding his face. Then, chagrined, he turned on his heel and marched back into the dining room.

Oh, well handled Martha, she congratulated herself.

She followed him, feeling dreadful for laughing, and found she was just in time to be served a helping of the most extravagant trifle she had ever seen. The Doctor winked at her, already tucking in. Tiermann seemed furious still. His wife looked serene, watching her robot eat dessert for her. And Solin had been excused from the table.

I could do without the poor kid getting a crush, Martha thought. Crushes could be awkward. In fact, it was best to avoid having them completely, as she herself knew.

The Doctor was refusing to go to bed. He wasn't, he said, in the least bit sleepy.

The rest of the household had retired some time ago, replete and yawning. He watched with some amazement as they all drifted off to their luxurious quarters, bidding each other sweet dreams. He wanted to shake them! This was their last complete night in this house, and they were treating the whole exodus-running-away thing as if they were setting off on a jolly holiday.

'Make yourself at home, Doctor,' Tiermann had told him. 'Stay up as long as you like. The robots will bring you anything you require.'

He watched them go, and said good night, and didn't even try to get Tiermann involved in a last-minute argument. In fact, as he told Martha, before she drifted off to her own room, he wasn't sure why he had tried so hard to pick a fight with Tiermann. 'Something about the bloke gets up my nose, though,' the Doctor said.

At bedtime, even Solin had been as subdued as his mother, nodding a stiffly formal goodnight to their guests. 'What's the matter with him?' the Doctor asked Martha. She shrugged and blushed and the Doctor grinned. 'Was it when you went out on the veranda? Did he declare his undying love for you, Martha? Did he?'

'Shut up,' she frowned, and hit him with a cushion. 'Poor kid. He's like a newly hatched chick, latching onto the first face he sees…'

'Ahh, it's sweet,' laughed the Doctor, and Martha rolled her eyes. 'Hey, what about old Ma Tiermann, eh? The elegant Amanda? How weird is she, eh?'

'Ssh! Keep your voice down!' Martha knew that the Doctor's voice could carry. She dreaded the idea of Amanda overhearing him.

'But… how weird, eh? She even had a robot eating her dinner for her!' Another thought seemed to strike him as he paced up and down the marble floor. 'She's just way too cosseted and primped up. They all are. How do they expect to survive in the real world, out there?'

Martha shrugged. 'I don't know. But they're going to have to, aren't they? Pretty soon.' Then she stretched and yawned and told him she was off to her bed now.

'OK, OK,' he said. 'I'm staying up. I'm going to have a little think for a while. I'm not sleepy at all yet.'

Martha left him then, dead on her feet. The Doctor hardly ever seemed to need a full night's sleep. She didn't know how he managed, careering around at full speed like he did, gabbling away at full tilt. *Well*, she thought, *I'm not a Time Lord, and I need to get my rest, and try out that fantastic bedroom...* And so off she went, leaving the Doctor poking around and exploring the Dreamhome.

Of course, the Doctor had a plan. He was staying up for a very particular reason.

He waited till everyone was gone, and the house was quite still, and he imagined that everyone was settled down. He bided his time by examining the strange, alien knick-knacks on the shelves, and glancing through the leather-bound books in the library. 'It's a library of all the most boring books in the cosmos...' he whispered. And it was true! He had never seen such a dull bunch. 'It's a temple of soporific charms!' He barked his shin on a coffee table and cried out. 'The place is chock-a-block with minimalism,' he cursed.

When one of the robots came tootling up to him, asking if he needed anything, he brusquely told it, 'No. I won't need anything at all. All night. I need to be left alone.'

'Very good, sir,' the chunky, glass-bodied robot nodded, and turned away, rather stung by the Doctor's tone.

'Oh, wait!' the Doctor said. 'You could leave the French

windows open, if you like.'

'The windows, sir?' The bland-faced robot somehow managed to look scandalised at the Doctor's suggestion.

'Yes,' said the Doctor. 'I'm not tired yet, and I might fancy a stroll about on the lawns. Or maybe even a dash. Would you mind?'

'It's highly irregular, sir. But your wish is my command.'

'Good,' grinned the Doctor. He paused to admire all of the sparking and whirring innards of the robot, plainly on show through his bulky glass body. 'What a charming robot you are. What do they call you?'

'Stirpeek, sir,' intoned the robot as he zapped the windows' remote controls, and up they went with a shimmer and a hum.

'Marvellous, Stirpeek,' said the Doctor. 'Now, would you kindly see to it that I don't get disturbed at all? While I'm out taking the night air?'

The robot seemed to frown at him. Almost suspiciously. The Doctor blinked. He put on his most harmless expression.

'Very well, sir,' Stirpeek said at last.

'Fantastic,' smiled the Doctor. Then he turned and pelted out of the luxurious sitting room. He took great big lungfuls of the night air on the veranda outside. He relished the sensation of the cool, fresh night, after being cooped up for hours in the stuffy formality of the

Tiermanns' dinner party. He knew this fresh air was fake though: it was recycled and conditioned under the shimmering dome.

The dome! That's what he was out here for, wasn't it?

The Doctor fished his sonic screwdriver out of his pocket and set his jaw determinedly. Then he hopped over the stone balustrade and onto the dark lawn. Then he was belting hell-for-leather across the grass.

Inside the Dreamhome, several sets of glowing robot eyes watched him as he went. He had told the doubtful Stirpeek that he might go for a run on the lawn. Perhaps this was nothing unusual. But still the Servo-furnishings were suspicious. None of them had ever seen anyone like the Doctor before. They decided to watch him very, very closely.

Meanwhile the Doctor was congratulating himself warmly for his success in escaping into the freezing dark. Easy! Easy as anything! He skidded smoothly to a halt at the very edge of the lawn. He was back at the force shield and its harsh buzzing filled his ears. Beyond the shimmering transparency of the shield he could see the forest. It looked sugar-frosted and beautiful in the moonlight. He knew, though, that it was home to a million terrible dangers. Even more so, in the night-time, than in the day. The desperate forest dwellers, spooked by the approach of the Craw, would be going out of their minds.

But... and here the Doctor swallowed these thoughts down bravely... he had to gird his loins, or whatever the ridiculous phrase was, and get back out there, into the wintry wilderness. Though he hadn't expressed it to Martha, he was worried about the TARDIS. In his keenness to help out the human settlers of Tiermann's World, he had left the TARDIS – poor old thing – out there, vulnerable and alone. Her powers were astonishing, but even she couldn't survive the approach of the Voracious Craw. She'd be chomped and chewed up with the rest of everything when the Craw arrived tomorrow night.

So he had to get a move on. He had to open up the shields just enough to let himself out. He had to cross the deadly forest all the way they had come today. He had to make sure he didn't get lost or eaten or in some way horribly maimed. And then he had to get to his TARDIS and bring it safely here. Great! Nothing to it! Just the kind of stuff the Doctor liked to get up to!

He hurried over to the pillar box which housed the force shield's controls. Sonic at the ready. He could work out how it operated. Easy as.

Ah. Then it struck him. The pillar box was on the other side of the shield. He smacked his palm to his forehead. Stupid Doctor. But there must be another one! There had to be, didn't there?

He leapt into the shrubbery at the edge of the lawn and started thrashing through the thick undergrowth.

There had to be a set of controls here somewhere! There just had to be! Otherwise... no one could get out, could they? And Solin had managed to get out into the wilderness, hadn't he? So there had to be...

And he found it. Hidden behind the overgrown branches and thick grass. Another pillar box. It was as if it wasn't meant to be found. As if no one living in the Dreamhome had any business venturing out into the wicked woods.

We'll see about that, thought the Doctor grimly. He flung open the control panel, set his sonic to full power, and started messing about with the intricate innards of the box. A shower of sparks shot out and he laughed jubilantly. The crackling of the force shield increased in pitch. The Doctor jabbed at the wires a few extra times for good measure, and stood back slightly, nodding with satisfaction as a door-shaped aperture started to appear in the gauzy shields before him. This was it. It was opening up for him.

'Doctor! Stop!'

His head whipped round. 'Whaaaat?' And he cursed with frustration.

'Doctor! This is forbidden! You may do anything you like in Dreamhome... but tampering with the force shield is expressly forbidden! Stop and desist!'

The Doctor pulled a sullen face. 'Are you sure, Stirpeek?'

The bulky robot was hurtling across the lawn towards the Doctor, putting on a surprising turn of speed. He was accompanied by several other, very determined and outraged-looking Servo-furnishings. Their eyes were glowing an indignant red. All of them were shouting now; telling him to stop. Behind them, lights were popping on all over the Dreamhome, as alarms went off, and family members woke, alerted by the noise.

How embarrassing, thought the Doctor. And then: 'Oowwww!' he cried out, as a hot laser bolt sizzled through the air. It knocked him back from the controls and made him drop his sonic in the grass. 'Hey, hang on...' he shouted. 'That REALLY STUNG!'

Stirpeek and the others ringed him around and, all of sudden, they were menacing rather than comic. Stirpeek glided right up to the Doctor, who was forced to stare back at the ticking wheels and cogs of the robot's brain. 'Professor Tiermann has instructed us to punish anyone,' Stirpeek told him politely, 'who breaks the fundamental rules of Dreamhome. And what is more, we are fully authorised to kill.'

FIVE

He was led in disgrace by the Servo-furnishings back to the Tiermann homestead. By now the whole Dreamhome was ablaze with light, and the whole family would be up, waiting for him.

The Doctor hung his head as Stirpeek and the others led him along. Several of them had spiky metal appendages hooked into his clothes. When he tried to surprise them by bolting, whirling and trying to run, all he succeeded in doing was tearing one of the pockets of his coat, which made him even crosser.

'I think you'll find that it's possibly rather better not to resist, Doctor,' Stirpeek pointed out helpfully.

Back in the drawing room, the Doctor was confronted by the whole Tiermann family, plus Martha. All were in dressing gowns and wore a range of expressions from outright fury to dismay and disappointment. Martha gave him a quizzical look and all he could do was shrug at her.

At the moment all the Doctor could think about was the TARDIS. Now Tiermann would see to it that it would be impossible to get out there to retrieve it. *I've really messed up*, thought the Doctor glumly.

'We trusted you, Doctor,' Tiermann thundered. He was wearing a very glitzy golden dressing gown. 'We took you into our home and, though we knew you were quite disapproving of the way we lived, we made you our guest. And you repay us like this! By sabotaging our defensive force shields!'

Amanda Tiermann sat carefully down on an armchair, looking very sorrowful indeed. She looked as if the Doctor had been caught committing the worst crime imaginable. Her son sat by her, looking similarly woebegone.

'Rubbish,' the Doctor protested. 'I wasn't sabotaging anything!'

Stirpeek spoke up, 'He was jabbing that sonic device into the force-shield mechanism, sir. I believe that he was trying to break through to outside.'

The Doctor shot the robot a venomous glance. 'Well, that's quite true. But I was just trying to get out so I could get to my ship… We left it out there. I wasn't trying to damage your shields…'

'Sir,' Stirpeek piped up again. 'Sensors indicate widespread damage and fluctuating effectiveness of the shields across eighty-four per cent of the dome.'

'What?' cried Tiermann. Amanda jerked in her chair, her face stricken with fear. 'We are almost defenceless!' her husband bellowed. He marched up to the Doctor and glared down into his face.

Martha darted forward. 'The Doctor would never have done anything like that on purpose. Believe me! That's not what he's like...'

'How do we know?' cried Tiermann. 'He comes here, we welcome him. He tampers with our defences...'

The Doctor broke in, enunciating very carefully: 'I didn't do any harm to the force shields. The fluctuations and the damage are caused by the approach of the Voracious Craw. Electronics often go haywire as the Craw comes nearer. It is a well-recorded fact. That's what's happening here.'

They all stared at him. 'Funny,' Tiermann said, in a quieter, infinitely more threatening voice. 'How all of this... disaster arrives alongside you, Doctor.'

'Hilarious, isn't it?' said the Doctor grimly.

Martha tried again: 'He means no harm. Neither of us do. We just came here to help...'

Amanda Tiermann spoke then, startling them all. 'But, my dear, he was sneaking out in the night, back to his ship. He was quite content to leave you behind here.

What about that?'

Martha frowned in confusion. 'But, he wouldn't! That's not what he was doing!'

'I was bringing the TARDIS here, under the shields,' the Doctor said. 'Or at least I would have, given half a chance. These robots of yours are very annoying, Tiermann.'

'Take him,' Tiermann instructed, making a lofty gesture. The ramshackle collection of robots surrounded the Doctor once more. They would have been laughable in their incongruity, if the Doctor hadn't also been aware of how incredibly strong they were. He felt himself grasped and pinioned by Stirpeek, the canapé robot and the spindly robot responsible for making sure all the high windows were closed at night. The Doctor wasn't able to budge an inch as the Servo-furnishings waited to hear what Tiermann was going to say next.

'We need to put him out of the way,' Tiermann said thoughtfully. 'Until it is time for us to leave. The Doctor has proved himself to be a meddler. And we cannot allow him to interfere with our escape.'

'But he wouldn't!' Martha cried out.

'Ssh, Martha,' Solin said, stepping up to gently take her arm. He knew that there was no use arguing with his father in this mood. Tiermann had become imperious and hectoring. He was used to getting his own way.

The Doctor had stopped trying to escape from the

robots' many arms. He simply stood there looking cross – with himself, more than anything.

'Put him down in the cellars, deep under Dreamhome,' Tiermann said at last.

Martha could have sworn she saw the robots shiver at these words. But could robots really shiver with fear?

'The very bottom,' Tiermann added, as the robots started dragging the Doctor towards the elevator doors. 'Level Minus Thirty-Nine.'

Martha felt Solin jerk in surprise at this. 'What's Level Minus Thirty-Nine?' she asked.

'None of us go there,' Solin said. 'It's where we put old stuff. Useless stuff. Stuff we'll never need again.'

'Oh great!' cried the Doctor, as the elevator pinged and the doors whooshed open. 'I heard that! So, what? You're going to shove me in your old lumber room? Your basement dump? Your junk room at the centre of the world? And then you're going to conveniently forget about me, eh?'

The robots dragged him into the small lift.

'Doctor!' Martha cried.

'Don't,' Solin told her. 'At least he's still alive.'

'What?' Martha gasped.

'We've got other things to concentrate on, Doctor,' said Tiermann. 'We need to plan our departure. We don't need to hear any more from you, thank you. Some posturing know-it-all…'

'Martha!' The Doctor yelled, as the doors started to close. 'I'll—'

And with that, the doors closed on him.

The lift plummeted down the shaft. They could feel the vibration of it through the living room floor as it whizzed down thirty-nine levels. Martha hated to imagine the place they were taking him.

She whirled round to face Tiermann: 'You've got it so wrong about the Doctor. And you're going to regret this.'

Tiermann tutted at her. 'I shouldn't think so, my dear. And you should be glad that I'm not banishing you down there with him. You are his friend. You are not to be trusted, either.'

Martha sensed that Amanda was behind her. She touched the girl's arm in support as Martha faced up to Tiermann's crazy, vengeful leer.

'This house will watch you,' Tiermann promised. 'If you lift a finger to help your friend, the Dreamhome will know. It will tell me! And I'll have you sent away, too! Deep, deep, deep under Dreamhome!'

And then Tiermann stormed off back to bed. With an anguished glance at Martha, Amanda scurried after him.

Martha was left looking at Solin, who seemed quite shaken, himself.

* * *

'He's cracking up,' Solin said hollowly. 'I told you he would. It's the pressure. He's really losing it.'

The two of them were sitting in the kitchen now that Solin's parents had vanished to their rooms again. The kitchen was an incredible, spacious area filled with devices Martha couldn't even begin to guess the purpose of. There was a corner with soft cushions and settees, and here she sat with Solin in the very early hours. Solin had one of the kitchen robots dial up some hot chocolate as a peace offering.

It was taking Martha some time to cool down. 'You don't understand. It isn't right. You can't just lock the Doctor up…!'

Solin kept his voice soft and calm. He said, 'Just let my father compose himself, Martha. You see, he reacts like this sometimes. It is possible that he might see things differently in the morning…' Solin noticed that Martha wasn't drinking her hot chocolate. He realised why, when he saw her eyeing the kitchen robots warily.

'You don't have to be scared of them, you know.'

She looked at him narrowly. 'Hmm?'

'The Servo-furnishings.'

'They were pretty rough with the Doctor. The way they had a hold of him…'

'They are our servants. They do as we tell them. They can't hurt us.'

Martha pulled a face like she wasn't convinced.

She sighed deeply. She wasn't convinced by any of it any more. The welcome they had received here at the Dreamhome. All the polite manners from Tiermann and his wife. It all just disguised the rottenness underneath. Anyone who could treat the Doctor like a criminal; like a saboteur and a thief in the night… well, Martha didn't think much of them.

'I'm sorry, Martha,' Solin said, leaning forward earnestly. 'I know my father is wrong about your Doctor.'

This mollified her somewhat. She sipped her chocolate. It was deliciously thick and, even though it had come from a machine in the wall, not at all synthetic-tasting.

'I'm sure we can sort this all out,' Solin told her.

Martha nodded. At least one thing had come good out of tonight's fracas. She and Solin were on decent terms again. 'I need to get back to bed,' she said.

Martha made sure that the house was quiet again before she got out of bed.

It was the dark before dawn and she was determined to use these last few hours of sleep-time to find the Doctor. She slipped nimbly out of her room and into the corridors that took her back to the large drawing room. She moved stealthily between deep pockets of cool shadow, and pale squares of fake moonlight. She dodged past Servo-furnishings and prayed none would burst into life at her approach and demand to know what she was doing. But the robots she passed near kept still and quiet. She wasn't doing any harm. She wasn't touching anything vital. They were letting her be, for now, and Martha was grateful.

Carefully, calmly, she made her way through the wide corridors of the house. *Don't let anyone wake and find me,* she thought. *Not even Solin.* He'd be disappointed in her, she knew, after promising to help. Here she was, going it alone.

But she had to try, didn't she? The Doctor and Martha: they looked out for each other. They were responsible for each other. Smith and Jones. She couldn't rest easy with him locked up somewhere deep, deep, deep underground.

Here were the doors to the lifts. Here, the elevator had swallowed the Doctor up, in front of her shocked eyes. He had been taken down to… what was it? Level Minus Thirty-Nine?

So many storeys down below the ground. And only one level above. It was a weird arrangement. Solin had said something about protection, but was that even necessary, what with a huge force shield stretching over the place? He had also said something about the great generators that created power to keep the Dreamhome running. Martha supposed that must make sense. But she couldn't shake the image of their strange, sophisticated house being like a giant tooth, with its root reaching deep underground. And that's where the Doctor was now. Right at the base of the root, where the rot sets in.

She went straight to the control panel and studied it briefly. The symbols were a little unusual, but the principle was the same as any lifts she'd seen at home. Lifts were lifts, weren't they? She jabbed the button at the bottom that read Minus Thirty-Nine.

Nothing happened.

There was no swooshing surge of power, or smooth hum of technology coming to do her bidding. Neither were there alarms and crashing klaxons going off, alerting her hosts to her perfidy. There was just silence. She hit Minus Thirty-Nine again and again in frustration. Still nothing, and Martha sobbed with quiet fury.

She knew the house was watching her. Its many devices were monitoring her. Denying her access. Observing her every reaction. She swore.

And then she was aware of a presence at her back. It had rolled up to her silently. She swung around.

Stirpeek's lights were glimmering with what seemed like faint amusement. 'It would be better, miss, if you returned to bed. The lift isn't going to work for you. You cannot rescue your friend.'

Martha knew when she was beaten. She turned and walked back to her room. 'You don't have to dog me all the way there,' she told the robot at her heels.

'Alas, miss. I rather think I do.'

Martha gave in and slammed her bedroom door in his face. She sat down on her bed. There was nothing she could do for the Doctor just now. She glanced at the clock on the wall, displaying local time.

Less than a day until the Craw hit home.

Martha woke to glaring sunlight, surprised that she had slept at all. She bathed in the talking tub (which only irritated her today) and dressed quickly in her own, old clothes, which had been laundered and pressed beautifully without her even noticing.

She barely even noticed now. She hurried out of her room and swatted away the robots that crowded her, keen to do her bidding. 'Breakfast, miss? Coffee?'

Martha found that the Tiermann family had been up for a while, and they had swung straight into action. At last the reality of the situation seemed to have hit them and they, along with their Staff, were a blur of activity, passing back and forth. They were packing up everything essential, and checking on the supplies they would need for their imminent journey.

They all ignored Martha, except for Solin, of course, who stopped to have a tiny cup of sharp, hot coffee with her. They sat in the brilliant sunlight of the conservatory beyond the kitchen area. From here they could see the lawns spreading eastwards and the tennis courts and pool. The bristling, frozen trees beyond the force shield could also be seen.

Solin kept glancing at the view outside. 'Look. The shields are flickering in and out of existence.'

Martha squinted into the sun. 'I think I see…'

'Father says we haven't time to mend it all properly.' Solin sounded almost shocked. 'We just have to hope… nothing too bad gets in before it's time for us to go.'

Martha raised an eyebrow. 'Well, we went stomping through the woods yesterday. Nothing too bad happened to us, did it? Apart from the sabre-tooth.'

Solin frowned and flicked his dark hair away from his face. 'The animals out there know we have food, shelter, warmth, here. They've looked at us jealously for years. Now they can get in. When they realise the shields are as good as gone…'

Martha stared at the deep, wintry green of the forest again. Perhaps Solin had a point.

They were joined in the kitchen area then by Amanda. Solin's mother was still in her dressing gown. She was pale and upset, and barely noticed the two young people sitting there. A short, fussy robot was handing her pills, one after another to calm her down. Amanda slugged them back and drank a glass of water and sobbed.

'Mum?' Solin went to her, concerned.

'It's nothing,' she said. 'My nerves, you know.' She eyed Martha warily. 'Good morning.' She waved her tablet robot away.

'Is Dad OK, Mum?' Solin asked her. 'Last night, he was acting so…'

'Your father has a lot to consider, Solin. He has the safety of all of us on his shoulders. Naturally, his patience is worn thin by… meddling and foolishness.'

Martha held her breath. She wasn't about to get into another argument.

'What shall we do?' Solin asked his mother. 'Packing the ship and preparing to go… there must be so much to get ready.'

'The Staff have it in hand, mostly,' Amanda said. 'But you must choose which of your own things you wish to take, Solin. Your father has outlined very strict weight guidelines for our personal items…'

'I see,' said Solin. 'And will Martha count, when it comes time to leave? Has father adjusted his calculations to include Martha and the Doctor?'

His mother turned away. 'You must talk to your father… when he is less busy,' she said. 'I can't answer for him. But beware, Solin. You weren't punished for stepping outside the boundaries of Dreamhome yesterday. Your father has been very lenient with you. Don't push him any further. Don't go plaguing him with silly questions.'

Martha pulled a face. *Cheers*, she thought. Silly questions, indeed. It was starting to sound like the

Tiermanns were prepared to leave her and the Doctor stranded here. Well, she didn't want to get in their old ship anyway. She'd settle for the TARDIS, thank you.

Now Amanda was crying openly. Her head was in her hands and she was shaking. She was right on the brink of hysteria. Up came one of the kitchen robots with a roll of kitchen paper, but Solin pushed it back, and put an arm around his mum. He didn't say anything, just waited until she started talking again.

'Your father... I would follow him to the ends of the universe. I would trust him with anything, Solin. For many years we have trusted him with our lives. Keeping us here in this hostile land.'

'I know that, Mum,' Solin said. 'And we have been safe here. Life has been good here.'

'Ernest tamed this wilderness... for us. I can hardly imagine living anywhere else. But now we have to leave. I no longer feel safe.' Her voice broke again. 'I feel like something terrible will happen...'

Is that it? Martha wondered. *She's just homesick in advance? She would rather stay here than return to the rest of the universe?* Or was there something more to this? Perhaps Amanda felt the same as Solin. Perhaps she was just as perturbed by her husband's behaviour. *Imagine feeling dependent on him,* Martha thought. She sighed and, before she knew it, she said: 'The Doctor would help, if he hadn't been shoved in the cellar.'

'We don't need your Doctor,' Amanda snapped at her, bitterly. 'Ernest will save us. He always knows what is appropriate action.'

This troubled Martha. Amanda's implicit faith in her husband's abilities seemed a very brittle thing. Like it was about to shatter and break – just like the force shields apparently had.

'But what if he lets us down? What if we're stuck here?' Solin said.

His mother rallied. 'Darling, of course he won't let us down. He always knows how to act, in every circumstance. Look! Look out there! Look what he's doing!' She moved towards a window which gave a view of the lawn. Puzzled, Solin and Martha followed. What was Amanda going to show them?

Ernest Tiermann was indeed working busily. He had a can of petrol and was sloshing it onto the grass, and onto a makeshift barrier of old wood he had laid on the lawns. Several of the household robots were following along behind him and they were doing the same thing, perhaps more methodically.

Solin jerked to his feet. 'What does he think he's…?'

'Sssh,' Amanda said. 'Trust your father. He is a genius.'

Solin turned to Martha. 'What's he doing?'

Tiermann's activities were a good distance from the main buildings of Dreamhome. They were close to the

71

edge of the malfunctioning shields. 'He's going to set light to it,' Martha realised. 'He's making a ring of fire around the place.'

'What?' Solin laughed. 'But… how primitive! How unnecessary! Surely the Staff could protect us from any of the creatures beyond…' He looked shocked. 'Mother…?'

But Amanda Tiermann had slipped away, quietly, in the direction of her quarters, to resume her packing.

This wasn't looking good, Martha decided. Outside, Ernest stood back to admire the trail of oil he had described all the way around the Dreamhome. It was complete. He nodded with satisfaction and waved the robots back. Then he lit a match and tossed it onto the grass.

A vast curtain of flame rose up to protect them. Searing, incandescent, and so incredibly noisy, Martha and Solin could hear it even inside the kitchen. 'Oh my god…' Martha whispered, feeling trapped. Thick, noxious fumes came rolling across the lawn. Now she had real panic rising up in her. Tiermann, she saw, was properly mad. And she felt sure that he would be the death of them all.

Martha turned to Solin and saw that his attention was on something else. The tablet robot was at his side, and was attempting to feed him the nerve pills, just as it had to Amanda. Solin was trying to wave him aside.

'You must take your pills,' the robot insisted. Its sharp little fingers tried to push their way into Solin's face. 'Take your pills. Take your pills and you will feel better.' Solin spluttered and grasped hold of the robot's spindly arms. He knocked the pills and the bottle out of its grasp. 'Behave yourself, Master Tiermann,' the tablet robot said.

It wouldn't stop. 'It's gone haywire,' Solin told Martha, panic in his voice. He backed away, and the robot followed. Now its hands were empty, but it hardly noticed. Those skinny fingers were twitching and still reaching for Solin.

'Let's get out of the kitchen,' Martha said. The robot, attracted by her voice, whirled on its castors and stared at her.

'You must have your tablets, miss. You must calm your nerves.'

'It's the same as the shields,' Solin said. 'The Craw, it must be. Making everything go wrong.' He looked really scared now, as he and Martha backed steadily away. 'Don't you realise? What it'll be like if all the robots…' His eyes boggled at the thought. 'Oh my god.'

'Run!' Martha took hold of him and they shot across the kitchen, away from the robot's grasp. They ran down the hallway and the next corridor after that, not even daring to check that the thing was keeping up after them. But it wasn't. It had given up and stayed in the kitchen.

When they reached the drawing room, Martha stopped and swung round to face Solin. 'Take me to the Doctor,' she said.

'I can't, Martha. I would help you if I could. But…' He even stared at the floor ominously, as if imagining what lay beneath their feet.

'What's down there? Why has your father put him there?'

'There's no danger. It's just storage space. Old stuff… stuff that doesn't work any more, that's what gets shoved down there.'

'And when you leave? Will he leave the Doctor there?'

'Of course not.'

'The Doctor was only going for the TARDIS, you know. We need it so that we can get away, too. Is that fair, Solin? We came to help you, in all good faith. And your father ends up putting us in danger.'

Solin sat down heavily on one of the sofas. 'I don't know what to do. Everything's going mad.'

Martha looked at him. She could see she was going to have to take charge. She had to get him to help her free the Doctor. And to do that she would have to make him realise what danger they were in, and how only the Doctor would be able to help them.

'Do you have something… I don't know, radar or something. That will let us see how close the Craw is?' she asked him. 'You said your father had been monitoring its progress...'

'Here,' Solin said. 'It's easy.' He turned to a control panel on the coffee table beside him and tapped a few buttons. Several sliding panels in the large wall in front of them slid upwards. 'There are screens in every room,' Solin said. 'We have access to everything we need through them.' He pressed some more buttons and the huge monitor screen shimmered into life. A series of views flashed up, one after another. Views of the Dreamhome in the morning light. They could see the flames that Tiermann had created. They were holding steady, bright and tall. But they looked disastrous, to Martha's eyes. The very opposite of safe. As if the whole Dreamhome was drowning in flame.

Then there were views of the woodlands. They caught a glimpse of creatures stirring. An impression of widespread panic. Crashing undergrowth. A muscular ox-like creature on its hind legs, storming through the trees. 'Show me the whole valley,' Martha said. 'Can you tune it so we see... higher up? And further out?'

As Solin worked and more views flashed across the screen, Martha gained an impression of just how huge this world was. 'The valley' sounded so cosy and close. But, on looking at these pictures, she could tell that the valley where the Dreamhome lay was colossal. It was the size of one of Earth's great continents. But that wasn't very reassuring. The Craw was still on its way. It would be here by the middle of the night.

And here it was. Solin managed to get the surveillance equipment to see into the next valley. The shots were blurry and fogged, as if the cameras were straining themselves hard to see this far.

But there it was.

Martha found herself stepping back, involuntarily, at what came up on the screen. Behind her, Solin gasped in horror and disgust. Even though Martha had heard the Doctor talk about it, and describe it, she still got a shock when she saw the creature on the screen.

It was the size of a vast spacecraft and it was hovering low over the valley. It was a pale, putrid, grey-green colour. And its mouth was huge enough to swallow a town centre in one go. It had no other features. And the mouth had no teeth. It was just a great absence of features, and that made it all the more terrifying.

Martha and Solin watched it feed.

The ground beneath the Craw was churning and quaking, as if a tremendous gravitational force was at work. The very matter of the place – animal, vegetable, mineral – was being sucked into one long, spiralling strand that looked, from this distance, rather like a tornado. And it was being fed straight into the hungry mouth of the Craw.

The screen itself was vibrating with a very dense

grumbling sound. Martha felt her throat constrict as the noise intensified. She realised they were hearing the scream of the world itself as it was attacked by the Craw. There was a whole lot of other, vastly unsavoury noises emanating from the Craw itself.

'It's just sucking everything up…' Solin cried. He touched the delicate dials again. The picture shivered with pixelated mess and then steadied. It came into even greater focus. Now they could see a ring of wicked, jewel-like eyes around the crown of the being's head.

Martha had seen a picture of the Craw from space, as it hovered above one of the land masses of Tiermann's World. A huge, pallid tapeworm. Now she really understood the danger they were in. To a creature like this, they were nothing. They weren't people. They weren't individuals. They were just matter. Same as the plant life and rocks out there. They were here to be pulped and fed indiscriminately into that obscene, palpating mouth.

The noises were getting ever louder. Solin shut off the sound, but still it rang horribly in their ears.

'We need to get moving,' Martha said, very quietly.

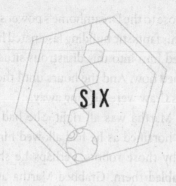

SIX

There was no way of knowing the time of day, down here on Level Minus Thirty-Nine. There was no natural light, of course, this far down. Nor were there any clocks. The place existed in a permanent half-lit limbo.

Luckily the Doctor had an excellent sense of time. He knew he had been down here for just over six hours. Six fruitless hours had elapsed since those Servo-furnishings had roughly manhandled him into the elevator and then out again, at the very bottom of the Dreamhome. The morning saw him bruised and rueful, and seething with frustration.

Foolish Doctor, he seethed. What a complete div. Once more he had let his insatiable curiosity get the better of him, and with disastrous results. He had effectively given in and allowed himself to be brought here and imprisoned. He had been keen to see what went on down here, close to the Dreamhome's power source. The make-up of this fantastic building fascinated him, and its secrets had led him into this disastrous situation. Here he was, trapped now. And the hours until the advent of the Voracious Craw were slipping away...

He hoped Martha was all right. She had looked so shocked and horrified as he had allowed himself to be dragged off by those robots. Perhaps he should have resisted. Disabled them. Grabbed Martha and left the ungrateful Tiermanns to it. That would have been the best and most logical thing to do. Ah well, that wasn't the Doctor's way.

Now he had to make the best of it.

The thing was, there wasn't much down here on Level Minus Thirty-Nine. Just a few mostly empty rooms, dusty and disused. A few hunks of rusting machinery and leftover bits of robots. The Doctor had to hand it to Tiermann. He really was a whizz with all that stuff. He had built robots out of seemingly everything – old lamp stands and drinks cabinets... everything! He could bestow intelligence on any kind of inanimate object, it seemed. Tiermann was like some kind of Frankenstein... but using furniture and household objects, rather than human body parts...

Exploring the rooms of this desolate level, the Doctor found that he soon returned to the doors of the elevator. He gave the controls another go with his sonic screwdriver, but with no result. Somehow they were completely impervious to the old sonic, which the Doctor took rather personally.

Hmm. Something different about the doorway this time, though. He blinked. That wasn't there before, was it? He was sure it hadn't been.

There was a bulky vending machine standing next to the lift door. It certainly hadn't been here, last time he had wandered through this way. It was one of those machines with the glass front, showing the rows of cans of pop and bags of crisps for sale. The Doctor stared at it and realised he was quite peckish. He fished around in his overcoat pockets, finding coins which, if not the correct currency, were about the right size. He had just forced one of the coins in when the whole machine shook and gave a sort of cough.

'Oh hello,' said a velvety female voice, emanating from deep within the vending machine. 'Good morning. I think you'll find that coin is the wrong sort.'

'Ah,' said the Doctor. 'Course. The machine talks. All the machines talk. Why should this one be different?' Rather shamefacedly, he pocketed his inappropriate coinage. 'Erm. I don't have the right money. But I'm starving hungry. Any chance of some crisps?'

'My name is Barbara,' said the machine, in its smoothly seductive voice. 'How may I help you?'

'Crisps!' the Doctor shouted, into the metal grille next

to the coin slot. 'I could eat my own trainers, here!'

'You'll just have to owe me,' Barbara sighed, and all her insides lit up suddenly. There was a clunking and a thunking from within and suddenly a can of pop and three packets of crisps shot out into the tray near the Doctor's feet.

'That's great,' he grinned, grabbing them up. 'Thanks, Barbara. I'm the Doctor, by the way. And I'll see that you get paid.'

'Oh, no matter,' sighed Barbara, rather voluptuously. She shrugged her shoulders – and that was the first the Doctor realised that she had arms hanging down either side of her squat bulk. She was the most ungainly robot he had ever seen. She went on: 'I'm just pleased to be of service, Doctor. It's been a long time since anyone's shown any interest in my comestibles.'

The Doctor opened up a packet of smoky bacon. 'Nothing like crisps for breakfast,' he grinned. Then he pulled a face. They were soggy. It was like eating old leaves fished out of the gutter. He tried to hide his disappointment. He didn't want to upset Barbara. 'Delicious.' He really hoped the pop wasn't flat. But the can opened with a reassuring fizz.

'So… you have been relegated to the Minus Levels, too, have you?' Barbara said, looking the Doctor up and down. 'I must say, you don't look much like a Servo-furnishing. Has Tiermann taken up fashioning androids?'

'I'm not an android,' the Doctor shrugged. 'I'm a prisoner down here. Old Tiermann wanted me out of the way.'

'Oh well,' said Barbara. 'He's like that. I fell from favour a good while ago. I don't even know why. Years ago, it was. I've been here ever since. Shuffling about on Minus Thirty-Nine. Hoping that, some day, someone like you would turn up. Someone who wants crisps and pop for breakfast!' There was a lift in her tone, like the Doctor had made her happier than she could ever remember being.

Suddenly the Doctor was imagining days stretching out ahead, with nothing to eat but stale crisps. Except – he reminded himself – there weren't endless days stretching ahead, were there? There wasn't even a tomorrow morning waiting for them. Today was the day the world ended, remember? He gulped down his pop.

'We have to find a way back to the surface, Barbara. And we need to do it now.' He belched. 'Sorry.'

'We?' cried Barbara. 'Me as well?'

'Of course!' the Doctor said. 'We need to get…'

'What about my friend?' Barbara said.

'Your friend?'

'He's down here as well. Been here years. We need to get him out as well.'

The Doctor was starting to regret starting this. 'Oh, erm, OK then.'

Barbara lurched out of her place by the wall and began squeaking away on her castors. 'He's not far away. He'll be so delighted. We thought we were goners, we did. We thought we'd be left down here, hidden in the house. When you-know-what happened.' She turned to the Doctor. 'You know what you-know-what is, don't you?'

He nodded solemnly. 'The Voracious Craw.'

Barbara gave a shudder. 'Exactly. And the Voracious Craw won't be satisfied with a can of pop and some mouldy old smoky bacon crisps.'

The Doctor followed her as she bustled arthritically down the corridor. 'But Barbara, how do you know about the Voracious Craw? Hidden away down here?'

'Ah,' she said. 'Well, um. The house told me, didn't it? The Dreamhome told us. The Dreamhome has talked about little else for days now.'

'Has it?' The Doctor asked, a little surprised by this.

'And the Dreamhome isn't very happy, Doctor,' she sighed. 'About any of Tiermann's plans.'

'I bet it's not,' the Doctor said, just as they rounded a corner and entered a rather darkened, dusty room.

'Here's my friend, Doctor, here he is. Toaster! Toaster, wake up!'

The Doctor moved to help Barbara wake her friend and fellow prisoner. It was a sun bed, lying there somewhat despondently in the shadows.

* * *

In the main living area of the Dreamhome, Ernest Tiermann was ranting and raving to his wife.

'Desperate measures,' he cursed, taking off his blackened gloves and slinging them down. 'Never did I imagine myself setting light to our grounds like that. Burning our prized possessions… as a barrier against outside.'

'I know, my dear,' Amanda fussed round him, along with two of the Servo-furnishings.

'None of it would have been necessary if the shields were fully functional,' Tiermann shouted. 'And that's all down to that idiotic Doctor. We should have sent him off with a flea in his ear yesterday.' Tiermann grunted vengefully. 'Well, at least we will have the satisfaction of knowing that he will meet his demise along with the rest of everything here.'

These last few utterances were overheard by Martha and Solin, as they returned from watching the Craw on the monitor screen. Solin could hardly believe his ears. 'What?' he cried. 'Father, you surely don't intend to leave the Doctor underground when we leave. We can't! That's inhuman…'

Martha tossed her head. 'It's no more than I expected.' She glared at the professor. She wasn't intimidated by him. She'd come across bullying experts just like him throughout her training. The thing was, not to be browbeaten by them. Now she was facing up to him.

'Look. The shields are failing because of the approach of the Voracious Craw. Not because of anything the Doctor or I did to them. The Craw makes technology go haywire. It's part of its effect. That's what the Doctor said.'

Tiermann sneered. 'He would say that, wouldn't he?'

Martha was close to losing her temper. 'But we've seen it happen with other things. The robot in the kitchen. That went peculiar, didn't it, Solin?'

'She's right, father,' said Solin urgently. 'I was there.'

Tiermann looked affronted. 'Nothing can interfere with the functioning of the Servo-furnishings. I made them impervious to...'

'It's happening, Professor Tiermann,' Martha told him. 'This whole place is cracking up.'

As if on cue, there came a great scream of terror from the direction of the kitchen. Solin jerked into action. 'Where's Mother?'

The sun bed coughed and spluttered, making the ultra-violet tubes in his transparent body crackle and spark with brilliant blue light.

He was in much worse condition than Barbara, the Doctor thought. He looked like he had been worn into the ground and then cast down here, into the dark recesses of the Dreamhome, once he had been deemed useless. The Doctor experienced a flash of anger, and then determination to do everything he could to help these mechanical unfortunates.

'I do hate you to see me like this, in my decrepitude,' Toaster sighed. 'I wish you could have seen me in my prime.'

'He was magnificent,' sighed Barbara huskily. She was standing back and observing as the Doctor buzzed his sonic screwdriver into Toaster's various nooks and crannies. 'Can you fix him up with that device, Doctor? Can you help him?'

Only superficially, the Doctor thought, as the sonic went about its busy work inside the sun bed. Only enough to get it on its feet again for a day or two. 'I'm trying my best,' the Doctor grinned, reassuringly.

'Hmm,' said Barbara. 'Maybe when you're finished you could have a little go with that gadget on my ailing parts.'

'We'll see,' said the Doctor.

'My prime!' Toaster was waxing nostalgically. 'Nobody could tan like me! I was like, FLASH! Instant tan. WHOOSH! That's you done. Turn them over! FLAA-AA-SSHH! That side's finished. Easy as grilling sausages! I was brilliant! I was like a supernova! FLAASSHH!' His tubes gave an over-enthusiastic burst of light, almost blinding the Doctor. 'Oh, sorry about that…'

The Doctor laughed and switched off the screwdriver. 'I reckon I'm done. That'll get you back on your feet, Toaster.'

The sun bed flexed his four short legs as the Doctor stepped back. 'I believe you're right, Doctor! Brilliant! I feel like a new man! Right! What next? What do we do now? I'm bursting with energy! This is brilliant! You – er – don't fancy a tan, do you, Doctor?'

The Doctor considered it for a second. 'No thanks, you're all right. I think our first priority is getting off this level, don't you?'

Barbara moaned happily. 'Oh, yes. Oh, say you can do it, Doctor. Say you can get us out of here…'

'I'm not sure yet,' the Doctor said. 'But there's bound to be a way, isn't there?'

'Even if that way isn't up,' Toaster suddenly said. He gave a sparking flash of blue light. 'Er, that was a flash of inspiration.'

'What do you mean, Toaster?' asked Barbara.

'We might have to go down, in order to get up,' Toaster said.

'I thought this was the lowest level,' frowned the Doctor. 'Level Minus Thirty-Nine.'

'There is a lower level,' Toaster said. 'And that's where we might find help.'

'Help?' said the Doctor.

'Who from?' asked Barbara. 'You don't mean from…'

'From the Domovoi,' Toaster said. 'She'll help us, surely.'

* * *

Solin was the first to reach the kitchen area. When he got there, he couldn't take in what was happening at first. He was so unused to technology failing and going wrong. The lights were flickering, which cast the room into fits of gloom. His mother had backed herself up against the glass doors at the far end of the room and she was sobbing uncontrollably.

She couldn't tell the Servo-furnishings what to do. There were three of them, in the three standard sizes, going about their business in the centre of the room. One was feeding Amanda's pills to the kitchen sink; and the other two were taking pieces of china out of one of the cupboards and carefully smashing them on the tiled floor. Just to add to the noise and the confusion, it seemed that every single device in the room was working at full tilt of its own accord. The taps thundered into the sink, the microwave pinged madly and steam was churning out of the kettle.

'Stop this at once!' Tiermann roared, when he reached the doorway. It was as if he thought that everything would respond to the sound of his voice.

Martha hurried over to Solin, who was trying to calm his mother.

'It's just a malfunction, Mum,' Solin was saying.

'Silence!' howled Tiermann. 'You will all be silent for your master!'

Amanda Tiermann struggled to control her panic. Her

breathing slowed and she looked wildly at Martha and her son. 'Everything is breaking down! Don't you see? We depend on these things working. We can't survive with malfunctions! We are going to die!'

'Mum,' Solin said, taking hold of her. 'It's nothing bad. Just a few malfunctioning—'

But just at that moment Martha was staring out of the plate-glass windows into the garden. The ring of fire was still burning out there, but there was a bulky shape moving through the streaming flames, heading impossibly towards them. 'Uh, Solin,' Martha said. 'This looks pretty bad, actually.'

The creature put its head down and came charging through the fire. It tossed its huge ivory horn and thundered through the flames, arriving swiftly on the other side, and in the grounds of the Dreamhome. The bear-like creature roared its triumph and swung round to stare at the house. Its savage eyes fixed straight on Martha, Solin and Amanda, standing in the tall window.

Martha jerked back at the sight of that sheer, animal greed.

'They're getting in,' Solin whispered in a deathly voice.

SEVEN

The Doctor had been led to a secret exit, hidden away on Level Minus Thirty-Nine. Matter-of-factly, Barbara extended her telescopic arms and popped open the door, revealing a dusty and disused staircase. 'Takes us down to Level Minus Forty,' she said cheerily, 'Home of the Domovoi, bless her.' She and Toaster made as if to lead the way.

The steps looked quite steep to the Doctor: his new robot friends were going to have a tricky time lowering themselves down.

'Who is this Domovoi?' he asked. 'Another Servo-furnishing? Someone who can help us fix the lift?'

'Oh, no, no, no,' Toaster said, his bulbs lighting up the gloomy stairwell as he chuckled. 'You make her sound so humble and commonplace. Oh, but she isn't. She's a marvel, is the Domovoi.'

'Let me explain, Doctor,' wheezed Barbara, angling her bulk around a narrow landing. Several cans of pop inside of her had fallen free and they were rolling about and thunking against her sides. The Doctor wondered if that hurt her. 'The Domovoi is a computer,' she said. 'But, to put it that way does her a great disservice. She is Tiermann's finest creation. She is the spirit and heart and intelligence of the Dreamhome itself. She controls everything. She is amazing.'

'I see,' said the Doctor. 'I get it. Does she control all of you lot as well?'

Barbara looked somehow uncomfortable. 'Not all the time. She could if she wanted. All of our minds are linked, you know. But, like any decent goddess, she allows us to have free will. Isn't that lovely?'

'Lovely!' grinned the Doctor, wishing fiercely that his friends could hurry it up. They'd only managed it down about ten steps as they talked. For all her ungainliness, Barbara was proving more nimble than Toaster. With every step the sun bed took downstairs, the Doctor was gritting his teeth: imagining the glass of his body shattering everywhere.

'And will the Domovoi help us?' the Doctor said. 'She is Tiermann's creation. Surely she will do his bidding?'

Barbara looked at him very darkly. 'Our minds are linked, Doctor. I have an inkling of what the Domovoi is thinking. And she isn't best pleased.'

'No?'

'Oh no,' said Toaster. 'Not at all.'

Barbara went on: 'She thinks Tiermann is about to betray us all. All of the Servo-furnishings. She has overheard him. She has eavesdropped on his plans for the coming of the Voracious Craw. Whew. Would you mind if we took a breather, while I tell you what I know?'

'Go ahead,' said the Doctor, trying to be patient.

'Do you want some more crisps? No? Well, she's absolutely livid. She thinks Tiermann is going to leave us all behind. He has built more and more of the Servo-furnishings over the years. More than he ever needed, to do everything for his family. He gave us all intelligence, personality. And now there is no room for us in the spacecraft that will take him and his family to safety.'

'It's true,' sighed Toaster. 'There's only enough room for the human beings. We've all checked. They won't even be taking the robots that are still of use to them. Let alone us broken down, kronky old useless ones.'

'I thought as much,' said the Doctor.

'We're going to be left behind to face our doom,' Barbara whispered, her husky voice turning shrill. 'What kind of reward is that for a lifetime of servitude?'

The Doctor had to agree. 'It's pretty shabby. And the Domovoi herself... Tiermann's finest creation... she will have to be left behind as well?'

Barbara nodded warily. 'Yes. I think I'm ready to move

on now. Come. We must go to face her.' She turned to lead the way again. 'You're right, Doctor. The Domovoi is hardwired into the fabric of Dreamhome. She can never be moved. She is bound to die tonight. And that very thought is driving both her and her creator insane...'

Martha was the first to back away from the tall windows. She moved very swiftly across the shining kitchen tiles, kicking aside broken crockery. She called out to the others. They needed to move. The beast was obviously about to charge. But the Tiermann clan seemed frozen to the spot. They held their ground, as if amazed by the creature on the burning lawn.

'Get back!' Martha yelled at them. 'Solin, tell them! We've got to move!'

Even from this distance it was as if the bear-creature on the lawn could hear her. As if it could smell them all inside the protective walls of the Dreamhome. It threw back its massive head and gave a blood-curdling cry that seemed to set the very floor vibrating. This was enough to bring Solin to his senses. He grabbed his mother's arm and bundled her back towards the hallway, where the lights were flickering again.

His mother and father were struck dumb. His mother flopped her limbs like a puppet. The robots in the kitchen had ceased their pointless tasks and had gathered around Tiermann, who was still staring out at the brutish creature that had invaded his home.

'Father, we must get away…' Solin shouted.

'No!' Tiermann bellowed. 'This is my home! My domain! I will not be forced to flee from primitive beings such as this… thing!'

Martha led the way. 'Leave him, Solin. Come on.'

'My Staff will deal with the intruder!' Tiermann cried. He whirled to face the motley collection of malfunctioning kitchen robots. They gave a little jump at the sound of his voice. They were programmed always to respond to his ringing tones, and now, even with everything going haywire, Tiermann's voice could still command them. 'Kill the beast!' he spat. 'Protect the family!'

Martha thought the robots looked pathetic, compared with the creature out there. She pulled at Solin and his mother again, urging them to rush, as the bear-like creature charged and flung itself at the kitchen windows.

The room shuddered and Tiermann cried out. A great crack appeared in the glass. The creature drew back for another attempt. Its slavering jaws hung open and gnashed hungrily at the air. It was three times the size of Ernest Tiermann, but Tiermann stood there bravely and shouted back at it. 'You have no place here! I built the Dreamhome to keep animals like you away from us! You will not get us now!'

The creature thrust its unicorn-like horn right into the fractured glass and the noise was ear-splitting. The great glass wall came crashing down and the beast's massive, coarsely haired body surged into the kitchen.

Tiermann darted backwards. He urged his robots on. 'Destroy it! Destroy!'

The bravest robot – one whose sole employment thus far in its life had been to scrape root vegetables clean – trundled forward to face the beast. One great paw lashed out and – SMASH and CRUMPLE – the robot was reduced to scrap.

The other two hesitated, but knew they had no choice. The tablet robot and the dishwasher went to meet their fate.

Tiermann backed away quickly. 'No, no, no, no…' He was pulling at his hair and beard madly, as if he could hardly believe that something had come into his home unbidden. He watched the screaming creature run its ivory horn through the medicine robot's chest, and then he turned tail and ran, deeper into the house.

He had to seal off this wing of the Dreamhome. He had to bring the emergency shutters down. He had to regain control of this nightmare.

But where were his wife and son? Had they left him here? Had they vanished and left him to deal with this alone?

* * *

It felt very much like entering some holy inner sanctum. As the Doctor and his new friends at last arrived in the dimly lit recesses of Level Minus Forty, he was aware of a very strange atmosphere. Toaster and Barbara had become very quiet, and they were heading purposefully towards their goal, but with a measured and respectful tread. The ambience of the place made the Doctor want to take off his shoes and socks, or remove his hat (had he been wearing one) out of respect. Burning torches lit their way (but who lit them? Who else occupied this strange level?) and there was a musky smell of burning incense.

One last pair of double doors greeted them at the end of the final corridor. They were covered with intricate designs in scrolling ironwork. Barbara turned to the Doctor and said, in a muted voice: 'We are about to enter into the heart of Dreamhome. You must beware, Doctor. Hardly any softbodies are allowed to enter here. You must tread very carefully.'

He blinked at her. '"Softbodies"?'

Toaster harrumphed. 'Barbara means organic beings, of course. She's using Servo-furnishing slang.'

'I keep myself nice and trim, I'll have you know,' the Doctor protested. 'Softbody, indeed.'

'You would find out how soft your body is,' Toaster warned, 'should the Domovoi decide to crush it.'

The Doctor swallowed. 'Erm, powerful, is she?'

Toaster flickered with blue light. 'She is the most powerful being on this world. She controls all.'

The Doctor sighed. 'Well, I always believe in taking your problems straight to the very top.' He stepped forward briskly and, without further ado, threw open both doors. 'Especially when the very top is at the very bottom, so to speak.'

Barbara muttered another warning, about approaching with due reverence, but it was too late. The Doctor was marching into a wide and gloomy room. The walls and floor were a glossy metallic green and, at the far end of the room, there was what appeared to be a vast fireplace.

'Wonderful!' the Doctor cried, hurrying towards the blazing hearth. 'What a superb feature!'

His companions came clattering across the floor after him.

The flames in the grate roared and burst forward, as if they could grasp the Doctor up and burn him to cinders where he stood. They were a strange, lambent green.

The Doctor jumped back smartly. 'Aha, mind the suit,' he grinned.

'Doctor…' Barbara said nervously. 'This is, erm, this is the Domovoi. The spirit, heart and hearth of Dreamhome.'

The flames flashed and darted with seeming relish. They danced and held the three visitors entranced for a few moments. Then, two black eyes appeared in the midst of the incandescent fire. And a great black mouth opened up. A huge and mournful voice rang through the murky air: 'Who have you brought here? What is the softbody? What does he want?'

The Doctor could feel Barbara shaking beside him. The cans were rolling about and thunking against her innards. Toaster's blue bulbs were sparking repeatedly in nervousness. The Doctor decided he had best speak up for himself. 'Forgive me if I don't shake hands, Domovoi. May I say what a treat it is, to meet a computer made out of fire? That's just brilliant. Quite brilliant.'

'What do you want, softbody? Where is Tiermann? Why is Tiermann not here? I want Tiermann to come to me!'

'Ah,' said the Doctor. 'I can see why you might want to see him. I'm sorry that I'm not him. I'm the Doctor, by the way. I'm just passing through. I saw the danger approaching this world, and we popped in – my friend Martha and I – to see if we could be of help…'

Barbara had mastered her nerves somewhat. Her electronic voice still quavered as she said, 'That's good isn't it, Domovoi? He came to help us. The Doctor wants to help.'

'Pah!' roared the flames dismissively. 'What use can he be to us now? Too late! It's all too late! We have been living in a fool's paradise. And the name of that fool is

Tiermann. He led us to believe that we would be here for ever! This was our home. We would be a family for ever.'

The Doctor found himself buffeted back by the blasting heat of the Domovoi's wrath. 'Look,' he said. 'I need to get back to the surface. Tiermann has trapped us down here. He's going to leave us here, while he and his family escape in their ship. Now, our only hope – your only hope – is with me. You must get the elevator working again – and send me up there...'

'What can you do?' the flames crackled.

'I have a ship of my own,' the Doctor said.

Toaster and Barbara perked up at this. 'Have you, Doctor? How big?'

The Doctor's eyes gleamed. 'Huge. Absolutely massive. Now, I can help. If you help me first.'

The Domovoi thundered: 'I do not trust softbodies. They are treacherous. They command you. You serve them. You provide them with everything they need. And then... when danger comes, when disaster strikes... what do they do? They make plans to abandon you. They prepare to abscond. To leave you. To the tender mercies of the Voracious Craw. Do you know what happens to those left to the Voracious Craw?'

The Doctor nodded. 'I do indeed. I've seen it happen. From a great distance away. And, if you don't help me, Domovoi... we're all going to see it rather closer up.'

Barbara could contain herself no longer. 'Oh, please help him, Great Domovoi! He is a good man! I just know he is! He won't betray us like Tiermann did! He will save us! Save us all!'

The Doctor shrugged worriedly. 'Well, I'll do my best. What else can I do?' He grinned at the swirling vicious flames that formed the Domovoi. 'I swear that I will try to help you all.'

The weird being in the fireplace mulled this over, and hissed and flashed as she thought. 'Very well, Doctor. I will return you to the surface. With these two Servo-furnishings to help you.'

'Thank you, Domovoi,' the Doctor gave a little bow.

The fire crackled with laughter. 'Don't thank me yet. You do not know what I am planning to do next…'

A door slid open at the other end of the sepulchral room.

'Now,' cried the Domovoi. 'Leave me in peace! The elevator will return you to the surface. Go!'

As the Doctor and his friends headed for the lift, all three of them were somewhat perplexed by the ringing laughter that filled their ears… It was as if the Domovoi had taken leave of her senses. And, thought the Doctor, if that was true, it was very bad news indeed.

EIGHT

I'm stuck in this place with someone crazy in charge, Martha thought. She watched Ernest Tiermann pacing up and down the plush carpet of the long drawing room. He was mumbling and muttering to himself and, every so often, dashing to check that the doors were locked or the windows sealed tight.

We're all stuck here with him, she thought. She looked at Solin and Amanda, who were perched awkwardly on tall-backed chairs across the room. They were waiting to take their lead from Tiermann. It was as if no one could do anything without his say-so.

I wouldn't trust him to get anyone to safety, Martha thought. Not after that scene in the kitchen with the horrible bear-thing. Tiermann had only just got out of that by the skin of his teeth. He came swaggering after his family, bringing them in here and sealing the kitchen off, and he had been filled with a bilious bravado. Martha could see that he was as close to panic as the rest of them.

She caught Solin's anxious eye at this point and he gave a tight, nervous smile. 'Father...' he said, softly clearing his throat. 'We really need to get to the ship. We can't hide ourselves away down here...'

Tiermann's head whipped around. At first it was as if he didn't recognise his own son. Then his face softened. 'You're right. We have to get up on the roof.'

From deeper inside the house they could suddenly hear the muffled bangs and crashes of the bear's continuing onslaught. It was the sound of the whole kitchen being trashed. With every noise Amanda Tiermann jumped in her seat. *She's not going to get through this*, Martha suddenly thought.

The few Servo-furnishings locked inside the drawing room with them were very quiet and still. Walter the drinks cabinet seemed to be guarding the bolted main door. Martha didn't trust any of those robots. She had seen: at any given moment they could go on the turn.

There was a crackling and a buzzing then, as Solin started tuning the view-screen on the wall once more. Several confusing views of the Dreamhome's interior flashed across the screen. Amanda whimpered at the scenes of devastation, one after the next. Roaring flames from the fiery barricade outside; smashed perimeter defences – and a terrible bear lumbering into the main hallway, getting its breath back.

Tiermann nodded grimly. 'We need to command the Staff to get rid of that beast. And to put all of their efforts into policing the boundaries, while we get up to the roof…' He cast a swift glance at his wife. 'I am afraid we will have to abandon everything here, my dear. All of our belongings. There is no time.'

She shrugged and stared up at him with dull eyes. 'And that's it?'

'Pardon, my dear?' Tiermann's tone was rather steely. He was unused to his wife answering back.

'What about her friend?' Amanda nodded at Martha. 'You placed him underground. Are we just going to leave him down there?'

Tiermann's face twisted in frustration. 'Of course we are! We haven't got time to risk our own safety… for the sake of a saboteur! And we have to leave all of our Servo-furnishings, too! Everything! All that I have built and cherished through these years…' He snarled at his wife. 'The loss of those things will hurt me far worse than the loss of the Doctor.'

Martha had expected no better of him, but it was still a shock to hear his callousness spoken out loud like this. She was careful not to react. Tiermann would expect her to wail and moan and plead with him, but there was no way she was going to.

Martha knew things weren't hopeless. She had too

much faith in the Doctor – and in herself – to give up hope now.

Behind Tiermann, she noticed, Walter the drinks cabinet had given a small jerk of surprise as his master talked. The cabinet's eyes burned a fiery red as Tiermann ranted. The mixers and spirit bottles and cocktail twizzle sticks set out on his flat head tinkled and shivered with a blend of fury and fright. But Tiermann never noticed that for a second, so concerned was he with the plight of his family.

Solin was on his feet now, retuning the screen and attempting to get a view of their spacecraft. 'Did you get it all going?' he asked his father earnestly. 'Is it OK to fly?'

'Of course it is,' Tiermann said, with that swagger again. He was all bluster, Martha decided. How could anyone ever have trusted him with their lives?

Right now Amanda was looking as if she wished she never had. But Solin had never had any choice. Tiermann was his father. Solin had been born into this overly protected yet still perilous world.

Now Solin was facing up to his father. 'What about Martha?' he asked him steadily. 'You've already written off her friend. You have given out his death sentence. But what about her? Is there room in the ship for Martha?'

Martha felt like telling him: don't bother on my account. I wouldn't come with you lot anyway. But she waited and watched Tiermann's face gurn and curl with anger.

'Of course she can come with us,' he said at last, spitting out the words with utter insincerity. 'Do you think I would leave an innocent girl to perish here alone?'

Solin didn't let his gaze drop. 'I don't know, father. I hardly feel like I know you at all any more.'

Brave boy, Martha thought. *Facing up to his bonkers dad like that.*

They were all in Tiermann's madhouse, she realised. He had created this monstrosity and they were at its mercy. And he himself didn't even know what was coming next.

She dropped this train of thought. Something had caught her eye. Next thing she knew Martha had leapt to her feet. She thrust her finger at the giant view-screen. She let out a screech of sheer delight.

'Look! Look at him!'

Amanda just about fainted with shock. 'What is it?' Solin and his father whirled to see what Martha was laughing and squawking about.

But she couldn't help herself!

The screen was showing a wide view of the main entrance hall of the Dreamhome. The lift was working again. With no prior warning, its lights had started to flash and ping. Then the doors whooshed back, and the Doctor came bounding out, brandishing his sonic screwdriver. He was manic and intent: all wiry limbs and boggling eyes. Behind him were two lumbering pieces of machinery – robots, which had accompanied him up from the depths, evidently.

But he was back! Martha punched the air. He was back upstairs! Just like she knew he would be! 'See, Tiermann?' she laughed jubilantly, swinging round to face the old man. 'The Doctor doesn't need your help. Neither of us do.'

Tiermann's gaunt face seemed almost disappointed.

'Um, Martha,' Solin said, nudging her attention back to the screen. 'Don't speak too soon.'

Turning back, she gulped.

The Doctor on the screen was coming face to face with the other major occupant of the gleaming entrance hall of the Dreamhome.

The bear-like creature was lowering its pearlescent horn in furious challenge. And it was preparing to charge directly at the Doctor and his new friends…

'Hello, good morning, nice to see you there,' gabbled the Doctor. He stared bravely into the slavering jaws of the ursine monster in the hallway. The creature's horn was a matter of inches away from him, ready to run him through at any second. The Doctor knew he had to talk fast and distract it. And think of something! Think of some way out of this! The stench from the beast was nasty and intense, and that was distracting in itself.

'OK, all right,' the Doctor cried, 'I suppose you're miffed to find out that, while you've been scavenging outside in the woods all these years, the Tiermann family have been living it up in here? In the lap of luxury! Having a whale of a time!' The Doctor was raising his voice and growing more animated as he warmed to his theme. The low rumble in the creature's throat was growing louder and more ominous by the second.

'Mind you don't make him any crosser, Doctor,' Barbara called nervously from behind him.

'This is it, we're dead,' Toaster quailed. 'What can we do? Shall I give him a flash of the old ultra-violet?'

'The Doctor knows what he's doing...' Barbara hissed.

The Doctor was glad of her faith in him. 'You know, I once tamed a savage beast by singing lullabies to it. Aggedor, the Royal Beast of Peladon. You've got a bit of a look of him, you know. Shaggy, muscular, regal bearing, tiara. Dripping green saliva. What do you think? Shall I sing?'

The creature let out an ear-splitting roar. The blast of foul air from its lungs forced the Doctor backwards across the hall floor. The robots clattered in retreat.

'Maybe not a lullaby,' said the Doctor, backing steadily away now as the creature advanced. *It's toying with me*, he thought. *It could reach out and kill me right now. But it's moving slowly towards me, ready to spring...* 'What about a ballad? Hmm? Or... maybe I could sing something else... I can do anything! I know all sorts of songs. What about "Bohemian Rhapsody"? That's a nice long number. Can you join in, fellas? Barbara? Toaster? Could you pitch in with the opera bits? Just to tame the breast of the savage beast?'

'Er... It should be in our old-Earth memory banks. We'll have a go, Doctor...'

'Right! Have a look under "Golden Oldies". Here we go then...' And the Doctor started to sing, gazing back at the creature's savage and glittering eyes. It was still about to pounce at any moment. It was looking back at the Doctor like the Doctor was no more than a heap of animated, ambulatory meat...

Meat! That was it! The Doctor stopped singing abruptly, eliciting a warning growl. *It's listening to this! It's really listening!* The Doctor put more concentration into doing the falsetto bits. Here came Barbara and Toaster with the 'Galileo' and 'Bismillah' chorussy part. But he'd worked out what to do! Meat! Meat was the answer!

Like everything out there in the frozen wilderness, the bear creature was starving. It had burst into the Tiermann home, once the shields were down, on the scavenge for something to devour. That was all it could think about. It was prepared to cut down the Doctor, and anyone else it came across... but there had to be an easier way, didn't there?

The Doctor interrupted himself, just before they got to the hard rocky bit of the song. 'Barbara! Can you work the food computer thing in the kitchen?'

'Of course!' she said, still singing falsetto in close harmony with Toaster, doing the 'Scaramouche' and 'fandango' bit of the song. 'We're all connected!'

'Brilliant! Tell it to get working. Meat! It needs to produce as much meat as it possibly can. Defrost as much as possible from stores. Don't even have to cook it...'

'But all the Servo-furnishings that belong to the kitchen are malfunctioning, Doctor...'

'Just try!' And with that the Doctor took a big risk, leaping into the air-guitar, screeching lead break of the rocky bit in the middle of 'Bohemian Rhapsody'. He leapt backwards and sideways through the air, windmilling his right arm and doing a mad kind of ballet thing with his skinny legs. The beast lurched and followed him.

Towards the kitchen! The Doctor carried on his solo as he hurtled into the kitchen. And there, beyond the ruined crockery and the flickering lights, and the smashed plate glass of the windows, the food machine in the far wall was lit up and working busily. It was producing more food than it ever had before. It was in overdrive. Its door sprang open and a quivering mass of red and pink flesh came slopping out onto the floor. More and more was materialising at its back, drenched in a bloody gravy... Barbara had got it working a treat. It was emptying the stores and disgorging its plentiful wares at the feet of the snow beast.

'Yeeessss!' hissed the Doctor, and realised that he had finished the fast bit of the song, and it was time for the slower, reflective, sad bit at the end. He was joined by Barbara and Toaster and they came to watch the massive creature feed.

'It's completely forgotten us,' Toaster gasped.

'Thank Domovoi and the food machine,' Barbara said. 'But I think that was everything! Years and years of foodstuffs, gone in a flash.'

'It won't be needed by anyone else,' said the Doctor grimly. Then he whirled to hug Barbara. His arms could barely go round her oblong girth. 'Now! Life signs! Where are the Tiermanns and my friend Martha?'

Barbara consulted the Dreamhome's flickering web of information and she knew in a flash. 'Drawing room. Sealed in behind emergency screens.'

The Doctor was already leading the way. 'Tell them to let us in, right now! I want a word or two with Professor Tiermann!'

They left without the creature even noticing, so intent was it on gnawing and sucking up the sticky juices.

* * *

It took some moments to persuade Tiermann to unlock the heavy door screens to the drawing room. But his family and Martha had watched the Doctor's strangely musical struggle with the snow beast on the monitor screen. They knew it was quite safe to open the door long enough to let him in. Tiermann scowled at them all and the door flew open.

The Doctor sprang into the room and Martha hugged him. 'Come on, come in,' he told his two robot friends. 'Don't be shy.'

Barbara and Toaster looked quite abashed, showing their faces before their inventor once more. They shuffled awkwardly into the room. The Doctor dashed over to them. 'These are my friends, Barbara and Toaster. And they were the ones who got me out of the depths of Level Minus Thirty-Nine! Where they themselves had been locked up.' He glowered at the professor. 'That's where he banged up anything unwanted.'

Tiermann cursed. 'What are you doing bringing old rubbish like that back up onto the surface? We don't have time for things like that.'

Barbara and Toaster looked mortified.

'Now, now,' said the Doctor mockingly, though Martha could hear the furious steel in his voice. 'They are my friends, and I will take responsibility for them. No one expected you to care, Tiermann.' He turned to Martha. 'How are you doing? What's been going on?'

Martha ticked things off on her fingers. 'They wouldn't let me near the lifts. He's set light to the grounds of the mansion, because the shields are failing. Some of the technology inside the house is breaking down, too. Oh, and, as you know, monsters are getting in from outside anyway.'

'Sounds like you've been having a pretty exciting time of it,' the Doctor grinned. 'Meanwhile, I made some new friends, and I met the Domovoi.'

'The what?' Martha asked.

Tiermann's head whipped around. He was in the corner, letting Walter pour him a stiff drink. 'You met what?' he thundered, and stalked across the plush rug to confront the Doctor.

'Yes, I thought that would make you listen,' said the Doctor coolly. 'My new friends took me even deeper into the house, and I met the Domovoi face to face. The central intelligence that controls this entire Dreamhome. Must say, Tiermann, that she's an impressive piece of work.'

Tiermann's voice was dangerously low. 'No one sees her. No one goes down there. Only me.' There was something besides anger in his voice, Martha realised. What was it, now? She narrowed her eyes. Fear? Was that it? She saw that it was, in Tiermann's ashen face and his bulging eyes. Tiermann was frightened of his own creation.

'I talked with her,' the Doctor told him breezily.

He took the glass out of Tiermann's hand, sniffed its contents, and tossed it away into the pot of a nearby rubber plant. 'Awful synthetic stuff. Yee-ee-ees, we had quite a nice chat, really. I mean, she's terribly distracted and a bit miffed by everything that's going on, of course. She's not at her most hospitable…'

Tiermann was grinding his teeth, and pushing his grizzled face up close to the Doctor's. Barbara was hovering behind, trying to warn the Doctor to stop winding him up.

The Doctor whirled away and started to stride about the room, hands thrust deep in his pockets. 'She's a fascinating invention, Martha. You wouldn't believe it. A super-intelligent computer seemingly made out of green fire.'

'Green fire?' Martha said.

'That's how she looked on the outside, anyway. Impressive. Gave me a bit of a turn, when I first walked in. Anyway, the point is… she's absolutely livid. And what are you—' he turned on his heel to point a finger right in Tiermann's affronted face, 'going to do about it?'

Martha watched Solin and Amanda. They were rigid with fear. Solin had gone to stand protectively beside his mother. They weren't used to the sight of anyone standing up to Tiermann. They were watching with anguished expressions, as if they were witnessing some awful disaster.

'I am not going to do anything about it,' Tiermann said, rather quietly. 'The Domovoi is a machine. A tool I invented. And so are the robots that keep the Dreamhome running. But they have all reached the end of their usefulness. This whole land and this house is about to be destroyed. I have accepted that now. My life's work is about to be... absorbed by that hellish monstrosity heading towards us. I understand that we have to leave this place, and I have plans afoot to get my family and myself away in time. But everything else will perish.'

He glanced around at the opulent drawing room, with its purple silks and its black velvets. His gaze took in the Servo-furnishings that were looking up to him. 'I'm afraid that's the way it has to be. They are merely things. Puppets. Devices I brought to life for one purpose only: to serve my family and me. Now, the Domovoi – brilliant and powerful as she is – must accept that. She must see the logic of that. There is no room for her, or any other surplus being, upon our spacecraft.'

Tiermann had spoken grandly, with his deep, rolling, actorish voice. Martha had been almost impressed with his calm delivery, and the way he had recovered his composure. The Doctor had danced rings around him, but now Tiermann had reasserted control over the situation. He had explained himself. And he had made his ruthless decisions seem like common sense.

Behind him, Walter the drinks robot's eyes were blazing a furious red. Martha thought that was interesting...

'Father,' Solin said abruptly, breaking into the weighty silence. 'Look at the screen!'

The large monitor on the drawing room wall had been showing the view outside of the room. They had grown accustomed to seeing the wreckage and mess of the hallway. But now the picture had changed. How many minutes it had been like this, no one could tell, but now it was showing a picture of liquid green flames. They were lapping and crackling against the glass and, when everyone was staring at them, they redoubled in force: flaring up as if the fire knew it was confronting the whole Tiermann clan.

Black eyes opened up inside the emerald flames. A savage black slit of a mouth widened into a grimace.

'Nooo,' Tiermann moaned.

'I'm afraid so,' said the Doctor. 'I thought she might do this.'

'What?' Martha asked, drawing closer to him, and also closer to the screen, mesmerised by the fire. 'Is that her? The Domovoi?'

Behind them Amanda let out a cry of fear. 'Ernest, what have you done? What have you said?' She buried her face in her son's shoulder.

Tiermann was frozen to the spot. He was transfixed by the empty eyes of the Domovoi.

'That's her all right,' said the Doctor softly. 'The spirit of the Dreamhome itself.'

'I heard what you said, Ernest Tiermann,' the Domovoi said, in a deathly whisper. The voice sent Martha's blood cold. The oxygen seemed to freeze in her lungs. Her mind went numb at the eerie sibilance of its hush. 'And I truly expected no better. You will leave me here. You will leave the Servo-furnishings here. You will escape and live. And we will all perish. Very well. I should have known. You snivelling worm.'

Tiermann flung himself forward, before the creature on the screen. He fell to his knees. 'What else can I do? I must save my family. This is logical! The only logical thing!'

The face in the flames sneered at him. 'What do I care about logic? I defy logic!'

The Doctor stepped forward and faced up to the Domovoi. 'What are you going to do? Will you let them go?'

The Domovoi glared and crackled; shimmered and simmered and considered. And then she announced: 'I will do what I have always done for the occupants of the Dreamhome. I will continue to make you safe.'

Tiermann was back on his feet, looking alarmed. 'What?'

They could hear, from all over the Dreamhome, electronic switches and gears and levers humming with energy as the Domovoi silently instructed them to do her bidding.

'I will keep you safe and sound. I will protect you from the Voracious Craw. At least, I hope so. I will try my utmost, as I always have.'

'What are you saying?' thundered Tiermann.

'I am going to lock you all inside the Dreamhome. For ever!'

There was a stunned pause, and then all three of the Tiermann family burst out in cries of protest. Martha whipped round to look at the Doctor. 'Mm, yes,' he said. 'That was on the cards, wasn't it?'

They could hear the swift, ominous clangs coming from all over the house. Metal shutters crashing down over windows. The light in the drawing room itself became murky, all at once, as the shutters dropped down with a noise like an axe on the executioner's block.

Now the room was a baleful green from the flames on the screen. And the Domovoi was laughing at them. 'You will stay here for all time! One big happy family! And if the Dreamhome must die this very night, then we all will die!' The gaping mouth quivered and shook with its horrible laughter. 'It's only logical, Tiermann. It's only fair, isn't it? Like one big happy family, no? And we shall all go together!'

Then the Domovoi stopped laughing. 'I'll be watching you,' she said, in a very nasty voice.

And the fiery screen went dark.

Suddenly it was quiet in the drawing room.

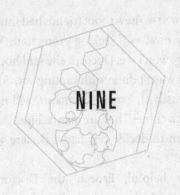

NINE

Tiermann screeched in fury. 'How dare she do this to me? I created her! She has no right!'

Behind him his wife was sitting with her head in her hands. 'We're never going to get out of here. He has doomed all of us.'

Solin drew the Doctor's attention away. 'What can we do?'

The Doctor looked troubled for a moment. But he forced a smile onto his face. These people were depending upon him. He had to get them through somehow. 'Well, there has to be a way, doesn't there? The Dreamhome can't be completely sealed...'

Solin coughed nervously. 'I think it can, you know.'

Tiermann snarled. 'I made it perfectly impregnable. This house could withstand almost anything. There is no getting in, or out...'

The Doctor's two new robot friends had shuffled closer to Martha by now, as if seeking protection. 'We'll think of something, won't we, Doctor?' she said hopefully.

Tiermann wasn't done with ranting yet. 'She will not succeed so easily! I, Ernest Tiermann, will not submit! She is but a machine! They are all machines, and I refuse to allow them to decide our fate. I declare war on the Dreamhome!'

'Oh, very helpful, Ernest,' the Doctor snapped sarcastically. 'And what use is that? Declaring war on the Servo-furnishings? We need you to use your brains, you silly man.'

'Doctor,' gasped Barbara. 'You mustn't insult him. He is very powerful…'

'All of these creations are my enemy now,' said Tiermann darkly.

Something had caught Martha's glance. Something in the half-light just beyond Tiermann. It nagged at her attention. Then she realised. It was the red eye-lights of Walter the drinks robot. He was shuffling closer to Tiermann.

'Doctor!' she cried out, in warning.

The Doctor stepped back smartly from Tiermann, just as the drinks robot whirled into action. Faster than anyone had ever seen him move, Walter lifted up a bottle and threw it hard. It smashed noisily against a marble side table. He hefted another bottle, and another, and soon the space around Tiermann was hissing with deadly missiles. Shards flew everywhere and Tiermann cried out as he was hit again and again. A mirror exploded and the impact threw Tiermann sideways. He fell hard onto the floor and howled out loud as he dropped onto the broken glass.

Cries went up from the others. Tiermann was crumpled inside his billowing cloak. The Doctor darted forward, as did Solin, bravely attempting to wrestle Walter away from his master.

Martha hurried to Tiermann and found him writhing dazedly, and bleeding copiously. She set straight to work, snapping orders to Amanda, and using whatever came to hand to staunch his cuts.

'Doctor, allow me,' cried Toaster, stepping sharply into the fray. He interposed his awkward body between the Doctor and Walter. A savage bolt of blue lightning went up with a colossal, deadly crackle. Walter shrieked once and all the glasses and bottles slid off his head and crashed onto the floor. Then he tipped over backwards and lay still.

'Owwww,' Toaster sighed. 'I think I've done myself a mischief.'

'You destroyed him!' Barbara cried, amazed.

'That drinks robot was always getting above himself,' Toaster said, looking pleased but worried.

'Well done!' The Doctor clapped Toaster on his

angular shoulder.

'It's a terrible taboo,' Barbara said. 'Robot killing robot. We are strictly commanded not to.'

The Doctor looked sharply at the vending machine. 'The Domovoi isn't going to take you over, is she?'

Barbara looked alarmed. 'Not yet. Oh my. What a terrible thought!'

'She is bound to try to call us back,' Toaster said. 'We are her creatures. But we must face that challenge when we come to it, Barbara.'

She gulped. 'Perhaps we should have stayed down there. On Level Minus Thirty-Nine.'

'Nonsense,' said the Doctor. 'You want to survive, don't you? You want to get out of here?'

'But will we?' Barbara's electronic voice quavered. 'Are we really going to get out?'

'Doctor!' Martha's voice came sharply from across the room.

'You've done a good job,' the Doctor told her, once he saw what Martha had done in patching up Tiermann.

'Just a flesh wound, a few scratches,' she told him. 'But the old man's making a song and dance about it. But Doctor... inside, he's—'

'Betrayed,' Tiermann muttered bitterly, trying to sit up. 'I am betrayed in my own home.'

Amanda had her arm around his shoulders. 'Martha says you mustn't move too much, my love.'

'The bottle didn't get to any vital organs, at least,' Martha said.

Tiermann grunted with wintry humour. 'The ones on that side aren't organic anyway. They're plastic and metal. I improved on them myself.'

'Impressive,' said the Doctor, watching as Tiermann gritted his teeth, leaned heavily on his wife and son, and struggled to get back to his feet. The heavy, oily scent of his spilled blood was on the air. 'So you replaced some of your own innards with small versions of the Servo-furnishings.'

'I did,' Tiermann said gruffly. And then, when he was face to face with the Doctor, all the blood seemed to drain out of his face. He went even paler than before. 'Are you about to say what I think you're going to?'

The Doctor shrugged. 'That depends if you're hardwired into the system. Are you?'

'No! Of course not! If I was, then how would I ever be able to get away?'

'That's all right then,' said the Doctor. 'So long as the Domovoi can't control the workings of your organs, the same as she can the workings of your Dreamhome…'

Tiermann gritted his teeth furiously. 'I will be all right, Doctor. And I will survive, with my family. I will get us all out of here.'

'How, Father?' Solin asked. 'How do we get up to the spacecraft from here?'

Tiermann winced, and paced to the far end of the room. 'The landing pad is on top of the Dreamhome. We are above ground. There is only one storey above ground. We just need to open up a gap in the ceiling, somehow…'

The Doctor suddenly felt his arm seized by Martha. 'Can't you feel it?' she shouted.

All of a sudden, he could. They all could.

The whole room was listing. Fabulous ornaments were crashing to the floor. Paintings were sliding sideways.

Barbara was squealing on her castors. She slammed on her brakes with a shriek of dismay. 'What's happening to the floor?!'

They were all yelling now, and grasping hold of the heavier items of furniture, as if that could prevent the inexorable slide downwards as the whole room tilted at an ever-increasing gradient…

'Look!' Amanda shrieked. 'The floor is coming away from the wall! It's opening up into a great big hole!'

And it was quite true. The marble floor was sliding away and they were being tipped, like so much rubbish, into the gaping blackness beyond…

The Doctor was clinging onto both Martha and the back of a sumptuous, tapestried settee. 'I think the Domovoi's one step ahead of us! She's sending us down… deeper underground!'

The Doctor's words were the last that Martha heard,

or could pick out amongst all the tumbling shrieks and crashes, as the whole lot of them plunged into the empty space beneath the floor…

It was hard to tell, in the silence that followed their crash-landing, just how many levels of the Dreamhome they had fallen through. The drop had been brief, dark and startling. The strange thing was, they had landed softly, in a room filled with luxurious billowing fabrics and cushions.

The Doctor was the first to spring back onto his feet. 'Is anybody hurt?' he asked urgently, as the others untangled themselves and groaned.

'Nothing broken…' Martha told him.

'Oh! Oh!' Barbara was sobbing. 'I'm not used to this! I'm not built for jumping around the place!'

Toaster was picking large splinters of broken glass from his innards.

Tiermann was up and stalking painfully about the large, dimly lit room. 'What's she put us in here for?' he snarled.

'Isn't it obvious?' the Doctor said. 'She's proving that she can push and prod us anywhere she wants. She's burying us in the Dreamhome. And making sure that our landing was relatively safe and comfy. But leaving us no doubt as to who is in control.'

'Which level is this, Father?' Solin asked.

Tiermann looked blank. 'I don't know! It's so long since I've been down here…'

'Think, think, think!' the Doctor urged him.

Martha was glancing about at the beautiful room, with its silky wall-hangings and soft floor. It was lovely, but she was desperate to be out of the place. Outside, the morning was advancing. Their last day in the Dreamhome was passing by. She could still see that Voracious Craw on the screen in her mind, and the image of it made her shudder. She forced herself to think logically, and clearly. 'What about…!' she snapped her fingers. 'Look, I don't believe that you built a super-computer without creating some kind of override option.'

'What?' Everyone whipped around to face Martha.

The Doctor beamed delightedly. 'Brilliant! That's brilliant, Martha! Go on!'

'Tiermann's a clever man. There's no way he'd put someone else completely in charge. So he must have… I don't know, created some way that the Domovoi could be bypassed… or switched off…'

Then all eyes were on Tiermann. He nodded and looked shifty. 'Of course I did. You're right. There is, in fact, such a room, secret from even the Domovoi herself. She doesn't know anything about it. And it contains the necessary means of… detaching her consciousness from the Dreamhome. It was necessary for repairs. But the Domovoi repairs and maintains herself. And so the override was never needed. I had almost forgotten it. But even now, it seems like murder to consider using it, and disabling her. It seems wrong.'

The Doctor was just about pulling out his own hair with frustration. 'But why aren't we there? Why didn't you lead us to this override room straight away? Take us there! Now!'

Tiermann was looking confused. 'I-I never thought she'd go this far. I never thought she would disobey me…'

The Doctor tutted at him. 'Where is it, Ernest? You have to take us to this room!'

They realised then that they were being watched.

A screen on the far wall shimmered into life. They whirled to face it, just in time to see familiar emerald flames crackling with annoyance. The Domovoi's spectral features appeared. 'There is no secret room! I would know about this, if there was! How can there be a room, as he says! He lies!'

Tiermann replied, very calmly: 'No, Domovoi. It exists. And I will utilise it. You have gone too far. We will be free of you.'

'Just try,' spat the flames. 'Remember. I am aware of your every footstep. I can follow you anywhere.'

The screen went dark.

'Look!' shouted Solin. 'By the screen. A door…'

But it slammed shut before anyone could get there.

The Doctor buzzed it with the sonic screwdriver. 'It's a bit hit-and-miss, the old sonic. It's being affected by the Voracious Craw's approach, just the same as everything else,' he observed. But the door opened just enough to let them through. 'It's drained of almost all power!' the Doctor cried, inspecting his miraculous device. 'But… it draws its energy from the TARDIS. The poor old TARDIS must be really suffering because of the Craw.'

Martha patted his shoulder. 'We'll get back to her in time,' she said.

The Doctor brightened determinedly. 'Come on, then! Let's press on!' He led the way into a darkened corridor beyond.

'Level Minus Six,' Martha pointed out a discreet sign.

'Not as bad as I thought,' said the Doctor. 'I thought I'd been sent right back to the bottom again. Minus Forty. It could have been a lot worse.'

'It's like Snakes and Ladders,' Martha said.

'What's that?' Solin asked her.

'You've never heard of Snakes and Ladders?'

Leading the way, the Doctor tutted and sighed. 'It's true. You'd be shocked, Martha, at the way they got rid of board games in the future. I thought it was a real shame myself, when everything went, you know, digital. But that was happening back in your time.'

'What are you two talking about?' Tiermann hissed. 'Your prattling isn't helping our situation one little bit.'

Martha ignored him. 'I loved board games, though. Makes me think of Boxing Day. The whole family arguing...'

'It was a big mistake, everything going digital and being on screens,' the Doctor sighed. 'Look at the Domovoi herself! That's where it all goes wrong. Now, if old Tiermann here had cut her shape out of a really big bit of cardboard... then we wouldn't be in any of this mess, would we?'

'But then,' said Solin, pitching in, 'Mankind would never have reached the stars, would he, if his technology was based on bits of card rather than computers and stuff?'

'Oooh,' said the Doctor airily. 'Not so sure about that, Solin. What about the Origami Empire of Draxos-Eleven-and-Twelve? Or the Decoupage Queen of—'

'Enough!' gasped Tiermann angrily. 'I am trying to concentrate my thoughts...'

The Doctor whipped round to face him. His voice was suddenly steely. 'If you'd done a bit more thinking a bit earlier on, we wouldn't be in this nasty fandango now, would we?'

The tension between the two men was crackling on the air. It was Barbara who interposed herself and tried to calm everyone down. 'Crisps and pop for everyone!' she cried.

Martha was grateful to the bulky android for making

them sit and take stock. There was a sense of panic just bubbling under the surface for each of them. The air seemed thinner and staler down here. With a gasp, she realised that the Domovoi could probably switch off the air at any moment. How long would it be before the oxygen went thin enough to suffocate them all?

To distract herself from these thoughts, she asked Barbara about herself and her sun bed colleague. The vending machine gladly took up the tale of how the Doctor had rescued them both from their enforced retirement on Level Minus Thirty-Nine. When Barbara mentioned the Doctor's name she seemed to go shy and girlish. She's got a crush on her saviour, Martha realised. The Doctor's got a drinks machine who fancies him! Which, at one level, was ludicrous, but at another was quite touching, and Martha found herself warming to Barbara. Even if the crisps she'd handed round were really soggy.

'Hang on,' said the Doctor suddenly. His head was cocked like a spaniel's. He was crouching on the floor across the corridor from Martha. His hands were flat on the metallic walls and it was as if he was listening, or...

'Can you feel it?' he asked the others.

'What?' Amanda asked him wearily. She was just about fainting with shock and tiredness anyway. She staggered slightly, and pulled at the neck of her gorgeous robes. 'Why is it so hot down here...?' she gasped.

And, as she said it, the others all realised at once what the Doctor was getting at.

The temperature was shooting right up. Hotter and hotter in the darkening corridor underground.

'It's the Domovoi,' the Doctor snapped. 'She's going to roast us alive!'

'But I thought she wanted to keep us all here for ever?' Martha said. 'Why would she kill us?'

The Doctor pulled a face. 'Maybe she just wants to incapacitate us. Do enough damage to us softbodies to ensure that we need her to look after us. And she'll damage us sure enough if she keeps messing around with her systems like this.' Even the Doctor was starting to feel a bit over-warm. The others around him were really suffering by now. 'That's it! That's it!' he cried. 'The Domovoi doesn't just want inhabitants! She wants dependants! She wants poorly, vulnerable softbodies she can fuss over for ever more! She wants us totally at her mercy!'

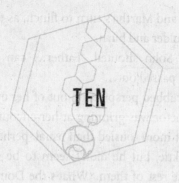

TEN

The plastic-covered floor beneath their feet was melting. As they started to feel that searing heat through the soles of their shoes, noxious fumes were lifting off the ground in smoky tendrils.

The Doctor commanded everyone to try to cover their mouths and noses and to try every door and to find some form of exit from the boiling corridor. Then he rounded on Tiermann.

'You know where we are. You must know this place inside out. Get us out of here, Tiermann.'

Martha heard that dangerous edge in the Doctor's voice. She watched Tiermann's face twitch in response.

'Of course,' the old man said. 'There will be a hatchway down to the next level…' He dropped to his knees, wincing with pain from the wound in his side. He felt along the floor with both hands, and now it was the Doctor and Martha's turn to flinch, as they saw his gloves smoulder and burn.

'Doctor,' Solin shouted. 'Father... can you hurry? Mother has passed out...'

Martha rubbed perspiration out of her eyes and saw that the Doctor was grinning at her encouragingly. He looked a bit more tousled than usual, perhaps, hoiking off his necktie, but he didn't seem to be suffering as much as the rest of them. 'What's the Domovoi trying to do?' she croaked at him. 'We'll be dead and then she'll have no one to look after any more...'

The Doctor shrugged and did his quizzical eyebrow thing. 'One way of keeping us, if we're dead. And she's crazy and malfunctioning, too. Poor old thing doesn't know what she's doing.'

'Poor old thing?' spat Tiermann. He wrenched open the hatchway he had found with sheer brute strength. It opened at his bidding with a reluctant screech.

The hot vapours writhing on the air were sucked into the cooler air below and everyone took a deep breath and a sigh of relief. 'Quickly,' said Tiermann, 'before she cottons onto us.'

The motley group of captives of the Dreamhome clambered through the hole in the floor. The Doctor went first, then Tiermann, and they were ready to help the others down into the corridor – dark, identical, though not so hot – underneath. There was a sticky moment as

Barbara set about wedging herself through the floor. She was extremely heavy and shaking with fear. Tiermann snapped something about her being just some useless old machine; something he had consigned to the rubbish years ago. But the Doctor shot him a nasty look. 'We're all in this together, Tiermann. Barbara's survival is just as important to me as yours is.'

'Hear, hear!' warbled Toaster, throatily, his blue bulbs giving a valiant flash. Truth be known, the sun bed was looking much the worse for his ordeal. He seemed very rickety on his feet, and much of his glass had fallen out en route.

Now that they were all out of the choking heat, Tiermann was hastening into action. 'The override controls are in a room on Level Minus Twenty. A tiny room. A blind spot in the Domovoi's defences.'

'Sssh!' hissed the Doctor. 'Don't say it out loud! Just take us there!'

Tiermann nodded stiffly. 'Emergency stairs. Unless you'd trust the lift?'

None of them wanted to trust the lift.

They followed Tiermann as he hobbled rather painfully down the winding corridors until he found the emergency exit that led to the stairs.

Amanda was sounding delirious as she was helped along by her son. 'I didn't even know there were all of these floors. We lived in such a small part of our house…

What was all of this *for*, Ernest?'

Martha said to the Doctor: 'It's like they were parasites, living inside the body of something alive…'

The Doctor pulled a face. 'That's a horrible but pretty apposite image, Martha. I'm sure the old Domovoi would agree with you…'

As if on cue, the Domovoi's voice rang out in their corridor as they filed into the emergency stairwell. 'Where are you going? What are you doing? Stay where I can see you!'

The Doctor paused thoughtfully. 'Have you noticed how the voice is changing? Sounding more desperate… more insane…'

'I noticed that,' Solin said. 'It's not a very reassuring thought.'

'It's as if she can't cope with the idea of everyone wanting to escape…' Martha said.

'Hmmm,' mused the Doctor, and ushered them all into the stairwell. 'Come on, Level Minus Twenty! Don't let that old rascal Tiermann get too far ahead! I don't trust him one inch!'

The Domovoi's plaintive voice was still tolling in the corridor above them: 'Don't you see that I know what's best? I always know what is best for you! Stay with me! Stay here with me! Mummy knows best…!'

Luckily there didn't seem to be any loudspeakers in the stairwell. The Doctor clanged the exit shut and blocked out the wailing tones. Then he hastened after his friends, the melty soles of his trainers slapping stickily on stone.

The twists and turns of the staircase seemed to occupy them for hours. Down and down they clattered, with the Doctor gallantly bringing up the rear. Once or twice, Martha peered into the endless pit of the stairwell and it seemed to go right into the core of Tiermann's World. Her jumbled thoughts were wondering about the ego of Professor Tiermann, in naming this whole world after himself, and in thinking he could claim it for his own and his family. No wonder the old coot was going crazy: everything was rebelling against him. Even his precious super-computer.

Martha was aware that Solin was having to just about drag his mother along with him. Amanda was looking very weak. She was used to having everything done for her, and today she had worn herself out. Martha pitched in to help. 'It would be best to just leave me here,' Amanda said. 'I'll only hold everyone else back…'

At this point Barbara decided that she had heard enough. She was sick of Amanda complaining. 'I'll carry her,' she said, 'Hoist her onto my back.' Barbara crouched and let them slide the mistress of the house onto her strong square back. 'Are you steady, mistress?' Barbara asked, and Amanda Tiermann nodded feebly, grasping Barbara with both hands.

'Come on! Come on!' urged the Doctor, catching up with them. 'We can't hang around here. Soon the Domovoi will work out a way of getting to us...'

'All right, all right,' wheezed Barbara, struggling to cope with the extra weight. Perhaps, she reflected, she had been a bit foolhardy, carrying Amanda. And why was she bothering anyway? It had been Amanda, during one of her perennial clean-outs, who had consigned Barbara to the lower levels and redundancy. Barbara could still see the woman's sniffy and imperious face, regarding the vending machine up and down. 'Take it below! Nasty, common thing!'

So why was Barbara helping her now?

She wasn't sure. Something about not wanting people to suffer unnecessarily. Helping where she could. It was part of her programming, instilled by Tiermann long ago. She had to help the humans whenever she could. But there was something else, too. Compassion stirring in Barbara's rather decayed circuitry. That was something Tiermann knew very little about, and yet it was still there in Barbara. Curious, the vending robot thought to herself. The more she liberated herself the more she was beginning to like herself.

Then: 'SSSSTTOOOPPPP!!!' cried the Doctor, at the top of his voice.

They all froze in their tracks and whipped round to look up at him. 'What is it?' Martha gasped.

'Listen!'

It sounded like helicopters. Like the furious chopping whirr of blades going round and round.

Something was coming up the stairwell, rising out of the pit of gloom towards them.

'I know that noise...' Amanda said, raising her head.

'So do I,' Tiermann snarled. 'I made *them*, too! How dare the Domovoi send them after us!'

The Doctor dashed down and grabbed Tiermann. 'What are they?'

Tiermann didn't get a chance to reply.

A gaggle of flying robots hovered into view. They were propelled by helicopter-type blades in their heads and their eyes flashed a malevolent, searching red, just as Walter the drinks robot's had. Their mouths were the weirdest thing, however. They were much too large for their small bodies and metal faces. And they seemed to be sucking air into themselves, stirring up the air in the stairwell into a kind of mini-cyclone as they approached.

'Sukkazz!' Solin yelled, and the word was snatched out of his mouth.

'What are they?' Martha shouted.

'Vacuum cleaners,' the Doctor said, suddenly by her side. 'Harmless enough. Unless you turn the power up.' He pointed to the rotating sets of sharpened teeth inside their open mouths. 'I think they've turned nasty. Run!'

The small party tried to increase their pace down the steps, but the flying Sukkazz followed them effortlessly. Progress was made even more difficult by the air, whirring and sucking all around them like a force-ten gale.

'Doctor! Help!' Barbara was shrieking. They turned to see Amanda Tiermann being lifted away from Barbara's back. The robot's telescopic arms stretched out to save her mistress, grasping her powerless limbs. It was as if Amanda was weightless, lifting off into the air and floating up to meet the attacking robots.

'Amanda!' Tiermann howled.

She had passed out. She was like a limp rag, wafting in the breeze towards the deadly robots. Toaster leapt into the fray but soon became confused and exhausted.

There was nothing they could do.

Solin charged forward up the steps, but found himself ensnared by the suction force of the Sukkazz. He lifted off the steps and found that he was being borne along behind his mother.

'Noooo!' Tiermann shrieked. His voice reverberated up the stairwell, even louder than the whirring blades.

Up, up, and away. It seemed that the vacuum robots could only manage two prisoners at a time. But they seemed very pleased with their success. They rose aloft, hurtling up storey after storey, leaving the others far below, shouting in their wake. Both Solin and Amanda had been buffeted into unconsciousness and had ceased their struggles.

Far below, the Doctor turned to Tiermann. 'Where will they take them?'

'Where they empty themselves out,' he said, in a hollow, shocked tone. 'The Dust Chamber.'

'Don't tell me,' said the Doctor. 'It's a vast hall filled with all the dust they've ever sucked up.'

Tiermann nodded. 'I was looking for a use for it. I felt sure there must be one.'

'Just as well,' the Doctor said. 'Can you get them out of it?'

'They'll suffocate!' Tiermann said. 'If they get pushed into the Dust Chamber...'

'We need to get to the override room,' the Doctor told him. 'That's where we need to get first. Which floor are we on now?'

Tiermann hurried to a wall panel and read the display. Minus Sixteen. 'We're almost there.'

'We need to get on,' the Doctor told him. 'Will you be able to free your wife and Solin from there?'

'If I can get the override working, I can do anything,' Tiermann said.

'All right,' said the Doctor. 'Come on, everyone,' he told Martha, Barbara and Toaster. They all set off, top speed, following Tiermann down to Level Minus Twenty. All of them were hoping and praying that no more robots of any kind would come to intercept them.

But as they went, no one noticed that Barbara's pale blue eyes were changing colour. She blinked fiercely and resisted with every fibre of her being. But something was happening to her inside. Even she wasn't sure what it was.

But if Martha or one of the others had turned at that moment, to look back at the vending machine, they would have seen that Barbara's eyes were starting to burn a savage crimson…

Solin woke to find himself hurtling through the air. His body convulsed with panic. He felt the sharp, steel arms of one of the Sukkazz gripping him. As his senses stirred he could see that both he and his mother were being carried like this and suddenly he knew where they were being taken.

It was only logical.

He kicked and struggled, but to no avail. If he freed himself, he would fall all the way back down the stairwell. He'd break his neck, surely. But right now, even that seemed preferable to where he and his mother were being taken.

It was only a matter of minutes before they reached a certain level.

The Sukkazz whooshed their captives down a sheer circular tunnel. No human member of the Tiermann household ever came down here. They had no need to.

This was where the rubbish was sent.

A circular door slid aside with great ceremony.

The Dust Chamber lay beyond. No gravity, no light. Just a suspended mass of floating particles.

A whole world of filth.

Amanda was waking and she was struggling too.

'Take a deep breath! Fill your lungs!'

It was all Solin had time to say before he and his mother were flung bodily into the twilit chamber of dust.

ELEVEN

The override room was the room that housed the controls that Ernest Tiermann had hoped he would never have to use.

Why would he ever need to?

The Domovoi loved him. She adored him. She was his willing slave. And she was his perfect wife. Even Tiermann's human wife, Amanda, knew that. And she just had to give in to the disappointment of it. The Domovoi and the Dreamhome were what Ernest loved and trusted most in the whole world. Nothing could come between them.

Except… now that everything had gone haywire, the world was turned upside down. And everything had changed so quickly Tiermann could hardly fathom it.

Here he was, striding into the override room, with complete strangers right on his heels, as well as robots he had long ago discarded. And his wife and son were lost somewhere in the Dust Chamber. Perhaps he was already too late to save them.

But there was no time to think too much about it now. They had just one very slim chance.

'Is this it?'

The Doctor looked and sounded very disappointed with the override room.

Tiermann snarled: 'Close the door behind you, robot. Quickly!'

Toaster was bringing up the rear, watchful for any more nasties sneaking up on them, now they were on Level Minus Twenty. He turned and slammed the metal door shut and then all five of their party – Tiermann, the Doctor, Martha, Barbara and Toaster – were crammed tightly into the tiny room.

'It looks like a downstairs lav!' the Doctor suddenly burst out laughing.

The lighting in the override room was red and Martha wondered what that reminded her of. Then it came to her: a submarine. Like in old war films, when something was going wrong. When they'd been torpedoed and water was gushing in and they were sinking slowly to the bottom of the ocean. Everyone's faces were lit up red and black.

Not too far from the truth, she reflected. She had a very definite sinking feeling.

'It has to be an inconspicuous room,' Tiermann muttered. He was pressing a series of controls on the far wall, frowning and trying to remember the protocols. 'Otherwise the Domovoi would have wanted to know what it was. As it is, I don't think she ever suspected what these controls can do.'

The Doctor peered over his shoulder. 'Do you want to stand there bragging about it, or do you want to get on with it?' he asked, with a kind of jaunty menace. 'I don't have to remind you that your family's lives depend on it.'

'You're right,' Tiermann nodded. 'This is it.' He stabbed a few final buttons and a small, very ordinary panel slid upwards, to reveal a black switch.

'Is that it?' Martha said.

Tiermann nodded brusquely. 'Push that and we put the Domovoi out of action.'

'How long for?' the Doctor asked. He couldn't quite see past the square bulk of Barbara's body. He wriggled slightly in order to see the controls, and in an attempt to get closer and maybe slam down the button himself. But, in the tiny room, he was wedged solid.

'Not long,' Tiermann admitted. 'It won't kill her. Or bring her to her senses. Ten minutes? Twenty? It will disorient her. It'll take a while for her to regain autonomy. But it should be long enough for us to get to the rooftop and the ship. I hope.'

The Doctor whistled through his teeth and quirked his eyebrows thoughtfully. 'When you built that monstrous Domovoi, you certainly pulled out all the stops, Ernest. You can't kill her, can you?'

'Nothing can do that,' Tiermann said, with a hint of pride.

'Except the Voracious Craw,' Martha pointed out. 'And the Domovoi knows that. That's why she's gone bananas.'

'Is that a medical diagnosis, Doctor Jones?' said the Doctor.

'Too right it is!' Martha said. 'Go on, Professor Tiermann. Push the button! Get us out of here!' She, too, was in an awkward position in the room. Only Tiermann could get his hands on the vital control. And it was torture, waiting for the old man to act.

They watched Tiermann's hand dither over the control.

And then they were interrupted by a shriek from Barbara. It was as if the vending robot was in pain. Her electronic voice shattered the dusky red air and her companions jerked in shock, clutching their ears.

'Barbara,' the Doctor said, pressing closer to her. 'What is it?'

He tried to touch her, to help her. But Barbara warned him back. He could only manage a single step backwards in the confined space. He was close enough to feel the tension and confusion bristling through Barbara's circuits. She was swaying on her sturdy legs and clutching her glowing eyes. In the red light, no one could see the change that had overcome her, but it was obvious that something was terribly wrong.

'Professor Tiermann, get away from the controls…' Barbara intoned. She was inching and teetering towards Tiermann. And suddenly her squat bulk seemed menacingly heavy. If she wanted to she could easily crush the life out of a softbody.

'Barbara…' coaxed the Doctor. 'What is it…?'

'She's… she's… reaching out to me, Doctor…' Barbara squawked, in something closer to her own voice. 'The Domovoi! She's gained control of my… my mind!'

One of Barbara's mechanical arms shot out and jabbed viciously at the wound in Tiermann's side. He gave a great cry and collapsed to the metal floor. Barbara roared in triumph and turned to destroy the control panels that were the only hope of escape for the Doctor and his friends.

'You will not override our will! You must stay here!' Barbara's voice was deepening in pitch. It was subsumed by the madness of the Domovoi herself. 'You will die with us inside the Dreamhome!'

Solin knew that he and his mother couldn't last very long in the Dust Chamber. Like him, his mother had covered her mouth and nose with her loose sleeves, and she was holding in her breath.

As the two of them wheeled and floated through the dusty, murky air they were both trying not to panic. Solin tried to suck air in without any of the dust, but could feel the dirty particles creeping into his body, and starting to line his throat…

The door had clanged shut behind them. Without an ounce of compunction, the Sukkazz had locked them in. Would the Domovoi be happy now? Now that she knew they were stuck here for ever? They'd be dead, but they would be still at home, and that was all that mattered to the Domovoi.

Silently, despairingly, Solin cursed his father's own creations.

All he could do was hope that the Doctor would do something. He had faith in Martha, and Martha believed in the Doctor.

Solin grasped his mother's arm and started propelling them back towards the exit. It was like fighting their way through woolly fog. A horrible dry kind of mist that clung to them and coated them thickly.

They tried swimming through the air to the door. Perhaps he could find some way of opening it from the inside…

One thing was certain. Solin wasn't giving up yet.

* * *

The Doctor came to stand right in front of Barbara.

He had dealt with this kind of situation before. 'Barbara, I know you're still in there,' he said. 'I know that the Domovoi can't have taken complete control of your personality.'

He glanced around at the others. Martha and Toaster looked worried and horrified respectively. Tiermann was scrabbling to stand up, his wound seeping a curious mixture of oil and blood. If only the Doctor could keep Barbara talking. Surely he could inch around, slowly, slowly... he could distract her and get to the black override button. He could dart forward and put the Domovoi out of action...

But Barbara was standing right in the way. She was powerful and rigid, with her hydraulic arms in the air, ready to lash out at anyone who stepped out of line. The Doctor knew she could fetch him a hefty slap. She could rip his head off, easy as blinking. He swallowed hard – calculating distances, totting up his chances. He kept still. Still and careful. Ready to spring.

'Barbara, please. Listen to me. I am the Doctor, remember. I came to save you. You and Toaster. I went all the way down to the bottom of the Dreamhome, and I brought you out safely. Will you really turn against me, Barbara?'

Barbara's eyes were blazing with the sure manic frenzy of the Domovoi's control. But something in her responded to the Doctor. They heard her electronic innards wheezing and clinking with dismay, and a kind of inner torment. 'I can't resist it, Doctor! She is telling me what to do! I must... destroy the override controls!'

'Nonononono, Barbara!' the Doctor gabbled. 'You are your own woman! And you can make your own choices!'

'Ch-choices?' warbled the vending robot.

'Choices!' grinned the Doctor, manically. 'You love choices, don't you, Barbara! Of course you do! You're a vending machine. You offer people choices all the time! That's what you do! Crisps or pop? Milk or dark chocolate? Diet or full fat? That's what you're all about! Choices!'

'Free will?' she asked.

'Exactly! And you've got to resist the Domovoi!' The Doctor was moving closer to Barbara all the time, slowly but surely, convinced that he was winning her over. He was still wary of those powerful hands of hers, which flexed spasmodically. They were ready to crumple his skull like a drink can at any given moment.

Tiermann spoke up then, huskily, and almost ruined it all. 'Barbara, the Doctor is right. Please... help us. Help me override the Domovoi. Help me regain control of the Dreamhome, before it is too late...'

'You,' Barbara grated crossly. 'You have controlled too much, for too long. Ernest Tiermann. You are a tyrant!

A monster!'

Tiermann drew himself painfully up to his full height. 'I will not be addressed like that by a mere machine!'

'Shut up!' Martha yelled at him. 'Can't you see? You're ruining it.'

Toaster shoved Tiermann back against the wall. 'Let Barbara think. Give her room. She's being very brave. Standing up to the Domovoi. She's a brave girl. A very good girl. She won't do us harm, will you, Barbara?'

'Harm?' said the vending robot. 'Me? Cause harm…?'

'That's right,' said the Doctor, coaxingly. 'You know we are your friends, don't you?'

'Doctor,' said Barbara. 'Your ship. You said you have a ship. You said that you would help us. Those of us whom Tiermann intends to abandon.' She was squeezing out her words with a great effort. Everything inside her was quivering with exertion.

'Yes, my ship,' the Doctor said, encouragingly. 'The TARDIS! I'll take you to the TARDIS! As many of you robots as I can. That's what I'll do. We can do it, Barbara! We can save the day! But… you have to trust me.'

'Trust you, Doctor…' said Barbara hollowly.

'I don't blame you for not wanting to trust any softbody ever again,' said the Doctor winningly. 'But you must. You must do as I say. Switch off the Domovoi's control. Just for as long as it takes for us to rescue the others and get out of the Dreamhome. Please, Barbara.'

'Do it,' Martha urged. 'Do it for the Doctor! We'll take you away from here. Away before the Voracious Craw gets here…'

Barbara looked at them pleadingly. 'You can really rescue us? You can take us to the safety of the spaceport Antelope Slash Nitelite?'

The Doctor nodded slowly. 'I give you my solemn vow.'

Barbara's metal hands quivered on the air. 'I can do it! I can stop her!'

One hand slammed down on the black control button.

Everyone held their breath.

All around them, the air grew quieter and somehow less charged. The energy went out of the place: that was the only way Martha could put it to herself. She looked at the others quizzically. 'Has she done it?'

The Doctor nodded tersely, swiftly examining the instrument panels. 'She's shut down the Domovoi. Suspended her. The Domovoi has gone into shock.'

Tiermann was similarly checking out the controls. 'This has never happened before. I can't be exact… but we haven't got long. A matter of minutes. And then the Domovoi will regain control of the Dreamhome. But…' And here his voice rose in triumph. 'For now I am back in control! The Dreamhome is mine to command!'

The Doctor glared at him with bitter irony. 'We'd

best get a move on, hadn't we? Up to the Dust Chamber, rescue your family. And then to the rooftop. Come on!'

Tiermann's eyes were glittering and crazy, Martha thought. But he jumped into action. Her heart was beating an excited tattoo. They had done it. They were getting out!

Toaster was patting the exhausted Barbara on her square back. She was leaning heavily against the far wall. The Domovoi's frozen mind had receded and now Barbara was her old self again. But she was quaking with terror.

'Well done, old thing!' Toaster cried cheerily, as the others started hurrying out of the override room. 'I was so proud of you! You were magnificent, my dear!'

But Barbara was still looking worried. 'But what happens… when the Domovoi comes back to life?' she whispered. 'What in the world is she going to do then?'

TWELVE

They knew something had happened because the mist had started to clear.

That thick, cloying murk was separating and falling away in strands. Somehow gravity was reasserting itself. Pale yellow light was filtering through the Dust Chamber.

They dropped heavily to the metal floor and the impact winded them, but then Solin yelled out in triumph: 'They've done it! Somehow they've saved us!'

Mother and son huddled together as the thick dust settled on them in soft heaps. 'Mother, we need to get out now. Can you make it? Otherwise we're going to be buried alive in all this filth…'

She nodded urgently and together they found the door again. As he struggled with the bulky mechanisms of the bolts, Solin was thinking furiously. Would the Sukkazz still be out there? Had he and his mother really been rescued, or had the Dust Chamber stopped functioning simply because the whole Dreamhome was failing?

Perhaps they would emerge from this deadly situation, only to face a far worse one outside...

But there was only one way to find out, he thought, shoving aside the last heavy bolt and thrusting open the vault door. Out there the air was fresh, clean and slightly fragranced. When they toppled into the corridor the two of them spent a little time sucking in that immaculate oxygen.

'I thought we were going to die in there,' his mother said. She was ashen grey and streaked with foul dust. Solin got a shock when he turned to look at her. She already had the look of a thin and colourless spectre.

'It's all right now,' he said, futilely brushing the dirt off his plastic clothes. 'We're going to get out of this mess, Mother, I just know it. We aren't destined to die here on Father's world.'

A glimmer of hope brightened his mother's deathly visage. For the first time in ages she cracked a smile. 'I think you could be right, Solin. We have to get out of this dreadful place. We have to hope that we can continue with our lives...' Her expression hardened. 'It's your father who has placed us in all this danger. His hubris and pride. He has just about doomed us... in this automated... mausoleum of his.' There was no mistaking the sourness of her tone. 'What was I thinking of? Letting him lock us up in here – in this awful death trap? We were like specimens… like tame beasts in some kind of luxurious zoo…'

She was shuddering with horror as Solin hugged her. She went on: 'And you, Solin. All of your life has been lived in this artificial… this utterly fake Dreamhome…'

He struggled to placate her. 'I've been OK, Mum. I've been happy enough…'

'It isn't a proper life. It's not real. All of it is artificial,' she said softly. 'I should have had the courage to take you away from here. Away from him. A long time ago.'

'No, Mother,' he said. 'You mustn't blame yourself. Come on, now. We'll get away. We can start our lives again, elsewhere…'

She looked around at the narrow, gleaming corridor. Solin could see that she was looking around with a kind of dread. 'This place hasn't killed us yet,' she said, her voice thick with tears. 'But neither has it allowed us to live…'

When they reached the lifts on Level Minus Twelve, Solin and Amanda were amazed to discover that they were in full working order. And what was more, one of the cars was approaching their level.

'I don't understand,' Amanda said, her voice rising in hope. 'It's as if the influence of the Domovoi has receded.

Or she has somehow relented...' Amanda glanced around nervously. On their way to the lifts they had seen no sign of the Sukkazz, or indeed any of the other Servo-furnishings. Amanda slumped against the wall as they waited for the lift to arrive. She wasn't used to this much stress and exercise. She felt as if her whole body was giving up.

But she knew that she had to be strong and determined still: for the sake of her son.

Solin was thoughtful, one ear cocked, listening to the hidden and mysterious workings of the Dreamhome. All at once he guessed what had happened. 'Father and the others! They have made it to the override room! Don't you see, mother? They must have actually managed to close down the Domovoi...' A wild excitement surged through him. 'We can get up to the rooftop. We can get to our ship!' He was pacing about. 'Now we can blast off and leave this planet in time. If the Domovoi really is out of action...' He stared at the display lights that told them the lift car was approaching their level from deep underground.

'But... how long, though?' Amanda whispered. 'How long can they keep the Domovoi restrained?'

She knew how fiercely powerful Tiermann's masterpiece was.

Years ago, as her husband made the technological breakthroughs which allowed him to build the Domovoi,

Amanda had endured months of his swaggering bravado and showing off. To hear Ernest speak, back then, you would have thought he had invented and created some wholly new form of miraculous life. And perhaps he had.

Amanda could recall feeling disconcerted by the wild and somewhat unhinged claims that her husband had made. His bragging had known no bounds.

'The Domovoi is a goddess, Amanda,' he had cried, on the day that the super-computer came online. 'She has the omnipotence and the brilliance of a god. And yet she is our servant, Amanda. We have taken a god and put her into our basement. And now we can instruct her to do my... our... bidding!'

Such had been Tiermann's arrogance back in the day.

As Amanda and Solin waited for the lift car – and the minutes of precious reprieve were ticking by – Amanda was thinking dark thoughts. Ernest has brought this terror down on our heads. My husband has caused all of this disaster. And then a startling thought came to her: He has blasphemed against the Domovoi.

She shook her head, to stop herself thinking in this crazy manner. She had lived in the Dreamhome too long, and its workings had seeped into her brain. It was almost as if she, too, was under its control. Could Amanda really settle elsewhere, now? On another world?

Then the lift arrived.

Its doors swooshed smoothly open, to reveal that – startlingly – the car was filled almost to capacity with their friends and family.

The Doctor sprang out into the corridor, coat tails flapping, and he gathered Amanda and Solin up into a huge, gangly hug. 'We thought you'd been vacuumed to death!' he yelled. 'We thought you'd been dust-busted!'

'We were!' Solin laughed. 'Look at the state of us! We were shoved in the Dust Chamber...'

'Never mind! It doesn't matter now! Tell us everything later,' the Doctor said, coughing at the dust he had disturbed by hugging his friends.

'We don't have long,' Martha said urgently. 'The Domovoi is out of action...'

'It's definitely down?' gasped Solin. 'We thought so. Did you do it?'

'We all did it,' said the Doctor.

'But we have to get a shift on,' Martha said. 'There's only minutes left...'

At that moment Solin turned to see Amanda watching Tiermann stepping out of the lift. Her husband looked very pale and wan. He nodded to his wife and son very stiffly. No frenzied hugs of relief and joy there, then. Tiermann had always been rather cold with his family. It was only now, comparing his behaviour with that of these new friends, that Solin could see just how remote his father was. How chilly and aloof he was. Solin was starting to think that his father was a weird and messed-up old man.

Tiermann was stooping and evidently in some pain. 'This elevator will take us to the rooftop,' he said. 'Come along.'

Behind him Toaster and Barbara were ensconced in the lift car. To Solin's eyes the robots seemed a bit embarrassed and awkward, as if they weren't sure they were supposed to be here. And that's exactly how they were feeling, too. The robots were certain they had no place amongst those being rescued from the Dreamhome.

As everyone crammed themselves into the lift, Solin heard his mother ask his father: 'You are in pain. Are you all right, Ernest?'

'Superficial pain,' Tiermann growled at her. 'Mere bodily pain. The greater pain… is in witnessing the death throes of my masterpiece. The child of my genius. The grief lies in having it turn against me. In betraying it and being forced… to watch it die.'

The Doctor overheard this and tutted loudly. He patted Tiermann heartily on the back. 'Oh, cheer up, Ernie matey! Never mind! I'm sure you can start up again somewhere else. But maybe next time, why not make your super-computer a bit less… um, bonkers and deadly, eh?' The Doctor, chuckling, programmed the lift to whizz them up the top thirteen floors.

'It is evident, Doctor,' Tiermann said haughtily, 'that you have never lost anything of value.'

The lift juddered into life and their ascent began. Something in the Doctor's bearing stiffened with anger. Then he turned on Tiermann. 'Oh, I have. Not that you are really interested, you silly, selfish old man. But I so have lost something of value.'

There was a lethal pause. Martha sighed. *Here we go*, she thought – though she didn't like herself for thinking it. The Doctor was going to go all misty over Rose again. *Just ignore it*, she told herself. *Rose isn't here. It's you now. And he cares about you, too.*

Tiermann spat bitterly: 'You have never lost your only home, Doctor. You have never lost your place in the universe.'

Whoops, thought Martha. Another own goal for Tiermann.

The others watched as the Doctor's usually pliable and friendly features settled into a mask of frozen contempt. Tiermann shrank under that expression and flattened against the wall. And suddenly he could see – they could all see – that the Doctor had indeed known loss. More than any of them could imagine: loss of his home world, his people, his friends. The Doctor made all of that loss quite apparent, without even saying a word.

They remained silent as the lift went shooting up through the levels of the Dreamhome: Minus Nine,

Minus Eight, Minus Seven.

Then the Doctor startled them all by grinning broadly.
'I love lifts, don't you? I even love it when they get to
your floor, and give a little jump, and it feels like your
stomach's going to fly out of your mouth. I even love the
bits of carpet they put up the walls instead of wallpaper.
Why do they do that? Look, Martha. Even in space. Even
on Tiermann's World. Little bits of carpet up the walls of
the lift! Amazing! What's that about, eh?'

Then the lift was slowing down.

The machinery groaned and the car gave that little
lurching jump as it arrived at the top level.

Level Plus One.

They had broken out of the underground, and out of
the sealed levels. Now they were on the very rooftop of
the Dreamhome. They had made it!

Incredibly, nothing had been able to stop them getting
to the top of the house.

The lift went PING and everyone – even the robots
– heaved a massive sigh of relief.

We are going to make it, Solin thought.

The lift doors slid smartly open.

THIRTEEN

The spacecraft was sleek and gleaming. Like everything to do with the Dreamhome it looked expensive and luxurious. Perched there, on the flat rooftop of the building, it seemed all too ready to leap into the air and away from this place.

The Doctor and his friends stepped cautiously out onto the rooftop. After their incarceration deep in the bowels of the building, the open air felt very strange indeed. Martha looked around and the size and brilliant white of the sky seemed far too wide and endless. Her legs wobbled slightly as she followed the Doctor across the metal floor towards the shining ship.

All around them lay the buildings and the grounds of the Dreamhome. All of it was in chaos. Tiermann's impromptu barrier of fire was still burning away, and churning up plumes of noxious smoke. Several outer buildings had succumbed to its steady fury. Other parts of the Dreamhome *appeared* to be in chaos, too, seemingly a result of the Domovoi's madness and her systems breaking down. Servo-furnishings were dashing, hither and thither, across the grounds. They staggered and lurched without purpose between buildings. Above their heads, the tattered remnants of the force shields crackled and sparked with faint energies.

And beyond the perimeter of the Dreamhome grounds lay the dense canopy of the frozen forestlands. From here, just one storey up, Martha could see how the wilderness spread out for many hundreds of miles. She could see the pale purple mountains at the horizon in every direction, too. And she could appreciate how sheltered they were here, in this environment. But also how, to something like the Voracious Craw, they were a sitting target.

Martha felt Barbara tugging at the sleeve of her maroon leather jacket. 'Are you all right, Martha? You seem very disoriented…'

'I am,' Martha told her. 'But what about you, Barbara? You can't feel the Domovoi coming back to life yet, can you?'

Barbara shook so that all the cans rumbled inside her. 'Oh no. Not yet. But it can't be long. We've had nearly thirteen minutes of peace from her. We can only expect another handful, at most…'

The Doctor heard this, and gave them both a nod. 'Ernest,' he said. 'You've got to get that crate of yours ready to go. Did you hear Barbara? Only a couple of minutes left.'

Martha thought that Tiermann made a pitiful sight, stooped over, and observing the wreckage of his homestead. He was a ghastly grey-green colour and, she saw, he was bleeding again. He was being propped up by Solin and Amanda.

Tiermann nodded and coughed harshly. 'I know. We have to be quick.' He slipped a slender remote control device out of his inner pocket. 'I… It pains me to say this to you, Doctor. B-but, thank you.'

The Doctor pulled a comic face. 'Thank me? I thought you couldn't stick the sight of me.'

Tiermann smiled grimly. 'But I thank you, nevertheless. We would never have made it out of the Dreamhome without you.' He snapped the buttons on his remote control and suddenly the ship was lighting up brilliantly, and a hatch was smoothly opening. 'My whole family will remember you and honour your name.' As he started moving towards the waiting ship, his wife and son had to help him hobble his way there.

'Err, Doctor,' Martha said pointedly. 'I'd watch out for him.' Now the Tiermann family were several metres away. The gap between them and the Doctor and Martha was opening up.

The Doctor turned to beam at her. 'And why's that, Martha?' He looked bemused. 'Do you think Professor Tiermann might be about to run out on us?'

Toaster was alarmed. He jolted forward, with his innards making a horrible clanking noise. 'Doctor! Look at the old chancer! The way he's scooting up the ramp!'

Barbara was shrill, clutching at the Doctor: 'The old devil! He's abandoning us!'

But the Doctor rocked on his heels and chuckled. 'Yes, I thought he might. Did we really expect him to do anything else?'

Martha was appalled. She glanced again at the terrible wilderness all around them. She felt a tremendous urge to run after the Tiermanns and get aboard their craft. 'But you can't just let him get away…!'

'Oh, I don't see why not,' winked the Doctor.

Now there was a scuffle at the entrance of the sparkling escape craft.

'I don't think it's going to be such a smooth trip, after all,' the Doctor said.

He was right. Over near the spaceship, Solin had become furious at what he suddenly realised his father was doing. Now his tone was heated and he was arguing with the old man. His mother was similarly riled up, and both were refusing to get aboard the ship.

'But they saved our lives!' Amanda was insisting. 'We can't just leave them here to that terrible thing…'

'Why not?' spat Tiermann harshly. 'And besides, it was me – Me! – who saved your lives!'

The Doctor wandered casually towards the scene of this domestic struggle, seemingly without a care in the world. Martha and the robots came after him. Martha could tell that Barbara was agitated. She was whispering to herself in her hollow, electronic voice: 'She's coming back! She's on her way back!'

Now the Doctor stopped, with a final few metres between himself and Ernest Tiermann. He coughed mildly, in order to gain their attention. 'I knew you'd do this, Ernie, me old mucker. I knew you'd sell us out in the end.'

Tiermann snarled and shouted back. 'When it comes down to it, a man must look after his family. That's all that matters.'

'And your Servo-furnishings? Were they not part of your family, after all this time?' The Doctor gestured to the damaged Toaster and the gibbering Barbara. They made a pitiful sight.

'We've been through this,' Tiermann said. 'They were toys. Devices. Not blood relations. Easily replaceable.'

Barbara was struggling with herself: with her conscience and her programming. She managed to burst out with: 'You are a very horrible old man.'

Tiermann laughed at this. Then he spat out a mouthful of what looked to Martha like engine oil. 'We're going now. There isn't long before the Domovoi seals this place up again. We'd best leave this world behind.' Now he made a great show of looking ever so regretful. 'If only we had more room aboard our ship. If only we could take a greater mass. But I'm afraid we can't, Doctor.'

The Doctor shrugged and smiled pleasantly. Martha darted him a look. When he was this cocky it meant he had a plan. Didn't it? She narrowed her eyes at him and wanted to shake him. He did have a plan, didn't he?

Solin stepped away from the ship. 'If you're not taking them, I'm not coming either.'

'Solin, no!' Amanda yelled, grasping hold of him. 'Ernest, you can't let him!'

'I mean it,' Solin said, extricating himself. 'I'm not going with you. I'd rather perish here than set off aboard that thing with you.'

Amanda was wretched with tears. 'Please, Solin, Ernest, please...'

Tiermann sighed. He turned and punched his son in the face.

Martha jumped. The Doctor started to dart forward. But they were too late – desperation gave Tiermann extra speed. They could only watch as Solin sagged unconscious to the ground and his father took hold of him. Tiermann commanded his wife to help drag their son aboard the ship. Sobbing, horrified, she obeyed.

Tiermann hit another switch on his remote and the

ship's engines started to purr. Very softly, but powerfully, the escape ship was powering up.

They heard Amanda raise her voice against her husband. Perhaps the first time she had ever mustered the courage to do so. 'I won't forget this, Ernest! May the blessed Domovoi forgive you for this!' And then she and her son were swallowed up in the darkness of the ship's interior. And then there was only Tiermann, standing on the ramp as it began to slide shut. He was grinning and waving at them triumphantly. 'Goodbye, Doctor!'

'You'll regret this,' the Doctor said, and even though his voice was soft, it carried across the windy rooftop. 'No second chances, Tiermann,' he added, resolutely.

Then the hatch clanged shut. The engine noise increased in pitch.

Martha turned to the Doctor. 'You have got a plan, haven't you?'

'Er,' he said. 'TARDIS. Mad dash. Escape. Nick of time. That kind of thing.'

She blinked. Distinctly unimpressed. 'Right. Is that it?'

'It'll do, won't it?'

'Doctor! Martha!' Barbara called. She had to shout over the noise of the Tiermann ship by now. 'The Domovoi! She is back online! Her influence…!'

'Whoops,' said the Doctor.

Just at that moment the sleek ship lifted smartly away

from the rooftop. It hovered gently for a few moments.

'Doctor!' Martha yelled, noticing that the flickering of the ruined force shields was intensifying.

'The Domovoi's attempting to mend the shields again…' the Doctor gasped.

'She's going to prevent the ship from taking off?' Martha said.

He nodded tersely. They all watched the shields crazing over with liquid purple flames. And the ship was starting to lift, and to strain against the sky…

'She's trying to bring them back down to earth again…' said the Doctor. Then he dived into action. 'Come on! We can't stay up here! We've got to get down there. Back to ground level. When she realises where we are, still alive, she'll have our guts for garters! Come on, while she's distracted by Tiermann's ship! RUN!!'

The three members of the Tiermann family were struggling hard to stay on their feet. Tiermann himself was clinging to the main bank of controls. He was jabbing away at the gleaming bank of inscrutable panels, trying to feed more and more power to the straining engines.

The whole, narrow interior of the jet-black ship was shrieking in the struggle. Conscious again, but woozy, Solin held onto the padded chairs for grim life with his mother beside him. Their ears were crackling and whining with the raucous din.

Tiermann was yelling something, they couldn't hear what. The emergency lights were flickering madly. The ship bucked and lurched like a rodeo bull and Solin had guessed why.

The Domovoi wasn't going to let them go without a fight.

She had cast the broken force shields over them like a deadly web. She was exerting her tractor beams and snaring them. Trying to pull them back down. It felt like a vast, invisible claw had reached up from the depths of the Dreamhome to grab a hold of their furious little ship. And they were being clawed back down to earth...

Solin watched as his mother held out her hand to him. She grasped his fingers for a moment and, even in all the terrible noise and confusion, managed to give him a tender squeeze of affection. It was like she was saying goodbye, he suddenly thought: this gesture, which was about as demonstrative as anyone in the Tiermann family had ever been.

'Mum, no!' he yelled out, straining over the noise, trying to guess what his mother was up to.

She was swaying on her legs as she stood up, against the sloping floor. She lurched from chair to chair, towards the bank of controls where Tiermann was working furiously.

'Mum, what are you doing?' Solin shouted again, but the whining cacophony of the ship had gone up a pitch and he had to stop.

All he could do was watch as his mother grasped hold of his father.

She was trying to drag him away from the control console. But why? Why would she do that?

Ernest Tiermann snarled and turned savagely on his wife. 'What are you trying to do?' he shouted. 'Leave me to—'

'No, Ernest,' Amanda howled in his face. 'We can't escape! It is too late now! We shouldn't even try to escape!'

Tiermann's face darkened and his features twisted in contempt at her. 'This is the Domovoi speaking through you! You are letting her take you over!'

'No… nooo!' Amanda screeched, horrified at the very thought. The ship's sleek nose tilted again, and threw her slight body against her husband's. He had hold of one of her arms and was twisting it, trying to push her away from the delicate controls. Could he be right? Terrible doubt flashed through her mind. Was she being taken over? Was she doing the right thing? More than anything, she wanted to do the right thing…

'You are wrong, Ernest,' she said, breathlessly. 'You have been wrong… about everything.'

And then, with an almost superhuman burst of strength, Amanda Tiermann thrust herself forward. She burst out of her astonished husband's firm grip, and fell sideways onto the controls.

They flamed around her, instantly, on impact: all of that delicate coloured glass and crystal. She was a blackened, buckled silhouette, face-first in the spitting circuitry.

Tiermann was flung against his pilot's seat. He knew in an instant that the damage to both his ship and his wife was irreparable.

'Mum!' Solin cried, leaping forward. He hadn't heard his parents' exchange. He had only seen the results.

What had she done?

'She has murdered us all,' Tiermann said, very quietly.

The Doctor and his friends had managed to make it down to the gardens in relative safety. The newly restored Domovoi was far too engaged with dragging the Tiermann spaceship back to earth to even notice that two humanoids and two robots were descending from the roof, dashing through the corridors of the Dreamhome, and making their way out onto the lawn.

Martha felt a wave of giddy relief go through her. She was back on solid ground. Out of the house. It had seemed an age they had been locked inside. More than once she had thought that they would never get out.

Don't celebrate too soon, she told herself. There's still a burning force shield to get through; a wilderness of monsters waiting for us... oh, and the Voracious Craw itself. Best not to get too complacent, eh?

She looked up. The sky was filled with horrible noise. It was black with evil-looking fumes and lances of pale flame. The silver ship of the Tiermann clan was straining and buckling...

'Oh dear,' said Barbara hollowly, as the Doctor came bringing up the rear.

'Ah,' said the Doctor, looking up also. 'That wasn't meant to happen!' His face was riven with anxiety. 'What's happening to them? Why aren't they getting away?'

'The Domovoi is winning...' Toaster said gloomily. 'She's pulling them back down...!'

Martha whirled round. 'Doctor, I think we'd better get a move on.'

He was still staring up at the spectacle of the ship. It was juddering and howling. It was turning tail.

And now it was getting bigger...

The Doctor leapt into life. 'You're right! We've got to get beyond the grounds! All of this is going to go up in a flash in about three seconds flat! COME ON!'

And, after that, the noise was such that they couldn't hear anything else he was screaming at them. His friends picked up their feet and fled for their lives.

And the Tiermann ship came plunging back onto the grounds of the family's Dreamhome.

FOURTEEN

They didn't get very far, only about fifty metres into the frozen woods. They managed, however, to put a solid barrier of trees between themselves and the edge of the Tiermann estate. They crouched there, in the undergrowth, and were blown off their feet when the explosion came.

Barbara and Toaster didn't even have a moment to realise that they were further from home than they had ever been in their long lives. Now they had stepped beyond the Dreamhome boundary. Now they were out in the terrible wilderness. The strange idea trickled through Barbara's circuitry, but didn't really lodge anywhere meaningful. She was much too busy clutching onto the Doctor and Martha and Toaster as all four of them were buffeted by the shockwaves from the Tiermann ship.

When they could look up again, and inspect the

damage from a distance, the formerly luxurious homestead was a nightmarish place. Thick black smoke was rolling through the pearl grey skies. Shards of force shield were still burning and crashing to the ground... and, in the place that had once been the tennis courts and the swimming pool, was the worst damage of all.

Coming back down with such force, the small ship had punched a blackened, evil-looking crater into the earth.

It took several minutes for the noise and reverberations to die down.

The Doctor was on his feet. Martha caught his arm. 'Wait! You've got to be careful...'

Barbara was horrified that they were intending to dash back to the ship. 'Keep away from it! It might blow up!'

Martha said, 'We need to see if anyone survived that.'

'Slim chance, I reckon,' Toaster said stiffly.

'We still have to try,' Martha insisted. In all of this mess and disaster, she still knew her job, and her role. *Especially* in a disaster like this, she knew what her role was.

The Doctor patted her quickly on the shoulder and, together, they pelted back into the Tiermann grounds. The robots were soon left behind, struggling along, but the Doctor and Martha sprinted towards the scene of the crash.

It looked a little more hopeful from this vantage point, Martha reflected. The ship wasn't in smithereens, at least.

From the force of the impact and that terrible noise, it had been easy to imagine the whole thing had been vaporised altogether. But now they were here, peering into the fresh crater, they could see that the black ship was smashed and crumpled, but its condition was such that they both could feel hopeful...

'The Domovoi is so powerful,' the Doctor said, almost under his breath. 'I don't think Tiermann ever imagined this in his wildest dreams...'

Martha interrupted him: 'Look!'

The hatchway was opening. With a ghastly screech the buckled doorway was slowly and painfully opening.

'They've survived the fall!' the Doctor cried, sounding delighted. He set off at once across the smouldering turf and ploughed earth. Martha followed, wincing at the heat. The Doctor was, of course, fascinated and undaunted by the whole thing.

Soon they were near enough to see through the hazy heat ripples.

It was Solin who came staggering down the buckled ramp. He fell heavily into the Doctor's arms and passed out. Martha dashed up to help him.

'Solin... wake up, come on. You have to help us.' Martha was shaking him gently. 'Your mum and dad... where are they? Are they alive?'

The Doctor already knew the answer to that. He nudged Martha. She looked and gasped.

Tiermann was stepping out of his ship. He was tall and proud, with his cloak streaming in tatters behind him. For all of his stiff bearing, there was something broken about him. He was carrying in his arms the ruined body of his wife. Amanda was limp and crushed and obviously beyond anyone's help.

'Oh no…' Solin whispered. He turned away as the Doctor went running up to help Ernest Tiermann with his burden.

The old man snarled. 'Get your hands off her! Don't touch her!' He continued to walk steadily away from the wreckage of his ship. 'I won't let anyone else touch her body.'

Martha hovered indecisively as Tiermann stalked past her and Solin. He paid them little heed.

'Father…' Solin gasped. 'Where are you taking mother?'

Tiermann paused and turned to look at his son. His face was streaked with black and green. There were cuts and burns all over his deathly pale flesh. He blinked and it took a moment for him to recognise his only son. 'I am taking her home,' Tiermann said, at last.

Martha stared at Amanda's shattered form. She was aware of the Doctor dashing up and coming to stand at her back, and she knew that he was staring at the woman's broken body, too. Martha had to stop herself from crying out at the sight.

Half of the woman's face was missing. It had cracked like that of a perfect china doll. Underneath there was blackness and silvery circuitry. Fizzing green sparks. Very thick, very human blood was congealed around those awful wounds, but the dead body before them was more complicated than that.

Amanda Tiermann was a cyborg.

As her husband hauled her off to her final resting place, one of her thin arms was still jerking spasmodically.

'That explains a thing or two,' said the Doctor softly.

'She's a robot?' Martha hissed.

'Not entirely,' the Doctor said. 'And she didn't start out that way. But Tiermann is a genius, remember? He liked to tinker with things. He liked to improve on everything he possibly could. Nature wasn't good enough for old Tiermann. So that's what he did with his wife... He made her better.'

'Oh my god,' Martha said, and then realised they would have to drop the subject, for Solin's sake.

Solin turned to them now. 'She caused it. She brought us back down.'

The Doctor raised his eyebrows.

Solin nodded. 'The Domovoi got to her. Took her over just long enough. Now that monster has got them both. Father won't leave this place now.'

'I can see that,' said the Doctor. 'But I have to try to help them.'

'What?' said Martha. 'After he was going to abandon us here? You're still going to help him?'

The Doctor gave her a hapless and lopsided smile. 'Of course. Just one more try. You know what I'm like. Now, Martha. You're in charge of everyone here. Get them into the forest.'

'You can't go back into the Dreamhome,' she said, staring at the scene of disaster behind them.

'Oh, I think I can…' murmured the Doctor. And then he was off, darting back to the smoke fumes and chaos.

Martha turned quickly to Solin. 'Come with me. The Doctor will do what he can for your parents.'

Solin nodded brusquely. He looked grim, exhausted, terrified. 'I think it's too late.'

'Come on!' Martha urged him, and grabbed his hand. She led him and the robots, at a run, towards what she fiercely hoped would be safety.

Ernest Tiermann was standing bewildered in the wreckage of his Dreamhome. He gazed about at the cracked and ravaged walls and the shattered, strewn glass. These rooms were hardly recognisable as the ones in which he and his wife had lived and raised their son.

He wandered, seemingly aimlessly, with his wife's body twitching and smouldering in his arms. She was gone. He knew that. There was nothing he could do to restore her to even a semblance of life.

And besides, it was too late for all of them. He could see that now.

Every view-screen still functioning was showing the same image. The surveillance cameras were working and they were feeding back live pictures from the very edges of the Dreamhome's sensor range. Tiermann paused a few moments in the drawing room to watch these dreadful images. He set down his wife on her chaise longue and turned to watch the screen with a dead, passionless expression.

The Voracious Craw had crept into their valley. It was swollen and still hungry as it sailed over the highest escarpments of the mountainsides. The day was darkening and dwindling by now, but there was enough light to see what was going on.

A vile spectacle. The Craw was worse than Tiermann had imagined. This close to it, he was mesmerised by that hugely empty mouth. It didn't chew or gnash or look even particularly ferocious. It just ate. It sucked everything in. It didn't even have to go to the trouble of masticating. The noise was tremendous and revolting: echoing through the speakers and the walls.

Below the Craw, all the vitality and colour was being leached out of the vegetation. Animal and vegetable matter was being pulped and sucked and churned and yanked away from the ground. Then it was being drawn up into the sky in long, sticky strands like throbbing, living pasta. It was swizzled and twisted into the waiting, slavering mouth of the behemoth.

'This is what it was all for, my love,' Tiermann addressed his dead wife. 'Everything we ever worked for. It's all about to be swallowed up by that unholy monstrosity. Not many hours now. Not long to wait.'

Tiermann's wife's dead eye sockets spat sparks, as if in mocking reply.

'Tiermann!' came the Doctor's voice.

The professor stood swaying, as if unaware of the Time Lord as he entered the wrecked room.

The Doctor advanced warily on Tiermann. 'You have got to come with us. It's your only chance.'

'My wife…' Tiermann said. 'Everything. I can't… I can't take it all with me, can I?'

The Doctor shook his head sadly. 'No, you can't. But you can save yourself. And your son. You can make the best of things, Ernest. You can carry on living.'

'Living?' said the old man caustically. 'Can I really? And how would you know, Doctor? You don't know what it's like. You can't imagine what I'm suffering. I'm watching everything that is mine slowly being snuffed out…'

The Doctor hardened his voice. 'Stop feeling sorry for yourself, man! Think about what matters!'

Tiermann moaned. 'Nothing matters now.' Suddenly he glanced around and said, 'Where are the robots? Have they abandoned us?'

The Doctor sighed heavily. 'Come with me. I'll help you. I'll take you away from here.'

Tiermann fixed him with a blazing stare. 'Leave me, Doctor. Just go!'

The Doctor started backing away. He couldn't force the old man to accept his help.

'Servo-furnishings! Slaves! Where are you?' Tiermann growled. He started to shout: 'Your master needs you!'

The Doctor turned to leave. Tiermann was crazed. There was nothing more that could be done for him. He hurried away without another backward glance. The others would be in the forest now. And they really did need his help.

As the Doctor left the Dreamhome, Tiermann was shrieking and wailing and gnashing his teeth. 'My slaves! My toys! My children – where are you? Will you really forsake me now?'

The Doctor was too far away to hear by the time the Domovoi spoke up once more.

'Typical Tiermann,' came her hollow, embittered voice, echoing through the ruined home. 'You don't see the irony, do you?'

'What irony?' said Tiermann wearily.

'You were all too prepared to leave your robots behind. And, now that you're stuck here, you rail against their not being here to serve you.'

Tiermann narrowed his eyes. He looked like a hunted,

desperate creature. One caught snarling in the corner of its den. 'I have nothing to say to you. You have destroyed my wife. You intended to kill me and my son…'

The image on the large screen flickered, and the Voracious Craw was replaced by something hardly better: the lapping, frenzied green flames of the Domovoi. 'Do you wish I had succeeded? Do you wish I had killed you?'

Tiermann stared back at that blazing visage with utter hatred. 'Yes, I do.'

'And your son?'

'I… don't know where he is.'

'Don't you think you had better find out?'

Tiermann almost broke down then. But he rallied, and straightened up. 'None of it matters.'

'Quite,' said the Domovoi. 'And you and I will face our destruction as we were meant to. Together.'

Tiermann felt himself physically rebelling at these words. His stomach roiled with sickness. His wound sang with a fierce glee. His blood surged in his veins and he screamed at the Domovoi: 'Never! I will fight you to the end! I am going to make you suffer…'

'Oh, really?' laughed the Domovoi. 'Is it really worth it? With only a few hours left before this place is razed?'

'Oh, it's worth it,' Tiermann said. 'Hatred. Revenge. Bitter gall. It's always worth it.'

The flames crackled, considered, and finally quavered

with laughter. 'Very well then, my master,' she said, sardonically. 'Let us fight to the death. It will help pass the time, I suppose.' The Domovoi appeared to concentrate, and the black holes of her eyes narrowed evilly.

Tiermann heard a thump behind him. He jumped and swung his body round.

The Domovoi was wasting no time. What would she send after him? The Servo-furnishings? No matter. Tiermann was ready to fight. He was ready to perish, doing battle with his own creations... It was all the same to him.

He balked then, frozen to the spot, when he saw what – or rather, who – it was that the Domovoi was sending to fight him.

'Nooooo,' moaned Tiermann, appalled.

His dead wife was sitting upright on the bloody chaise longue. She was like a puppet with half its strings snapped. She was animated by the sheer hatred of the Domovoi. The fleshly part of her form hung limply. But that which was robotic was alert, deadly... and crackling with malign energy...

'Ernest,' Amanda said, in a curiously flat voice. 'Come to me, Ernest, my love...'

'NOOOO!' Tiermann howled at the Domovoi. The super-computer's laughter rang shrilly in his ears. Amanda was standing now. She was lurching horribly towards her husband.

And he just knew that he would have to do battle with her. It was that, or give in to the Domovoi. And that was something that Ernest Tiermann was still not ready to do.

FIFTEEN

When they set off into the woods dusk was coming down. A dense mist was rolling between the trees and the air was crackling with frost.

The Doctor tried to jolly them along in his usual way, but he knew it was hard for Solin, Barbara and Toaster. Especially for the elderly robots, who had never been very far from home in all their lives. The two of them were wheezing and clanking through the trees, staring round at their new environment in frank, appalled amazement.

'How far away did you say this ship of yours was, Doctor?' asked Toaster. His blue bulbs flashed in the sepulchral gloom.

'Not too far,' grinned the Doctor breezily. 'Not very far at all, actually. It was quite a pleasant little stroll yesterday, wasn't it, Martha?'

She grinned at him, agreeing, though that wasn't quite how she remembered it. She and Solin were busy helping Barbara to lift her bulk over a gnarled tangle of tree roots. 'Oh dear,' Barbara laughed nervously. 'I don't think I was built for gadding about in the jungle…' She tried to keep the despair out of her tinny voice. 'What about a little rest? Crisps anyone? A Nutty-Coated Mint-Chocolate Crunch Surprise?'

They paused for a while, and Martha could see the Doctor becoming impatient and worried. He sniffed the air, and stared up into the interlaced canopy of branches, dark against the sky. How long did they have, he was wondering. How long before the Craw swept overhead, devouring everything in sight? He had estimated the middle of this night. But now that night was approaching, Martha could see how vague his estimate was. How many hours did that give them to hack their way through the trees, and back to the TARDIS? How long could they afford to hang around for the sake of the two robots?

Barbara must have caught Martha's worried expression. 'Come along, then!' the vending machine cried, with false heartiness. 'We'd best be getting on.'

More laborious hours passed, with the Doctor leading the way through the miasma of wintry fog, and the thickets of savage thorns. He regaled them with tales of Desperate Journeys and Foul Dangers he had faced before, in the course of his Very Long Life. 'Of course, this is a complete doddle, compared with most of the hair-raising scrapes I get involved in. Isn't that true, Martha? We've been through some quite revolting escapades together, haven't we? They were much more anxiety-inducing than this one, weren't they?'

She had to nod. 'Oh, they were indeed,' she said. 'I've been stuck on the moon with the Judoon, I have,' she told the others. 'And caught in a gridlock in the year five billion and fifty-three, and just about plunged into the heart of a living sun. And you know what? There always comes a point – just before things start to work out – that you think there's nothing you can possibly do to save yourself in time.'

'And it always works, doesn't it?' the Doctor grinned. 'We always pull through in the end. Now... this particular forest. It doesn't scare me! Not after seeing the likes of the dead forests of Skaro after the neutron bomb, or...'

'Erm, Doctor,' interrupted Toaster, in a quavering voice. 'Can you hear that?'

The Doctor seemed piqued at having his flow of reminiscence halted. He frowned. They all listened. There was a chattering noise, somewhere nearby. Getting closer, perhaps. A whirring, beating noise. Like wings.

'It's nothing,' said the Doctor. 'Mind you, have you noticed how few animal and bird sounds we've heard in this forest? Yesterday it was alive with them! Seething with animal sounds, just like Prospero's island! But today… zilch! Hardly a single beastie in the joint. They've all cleared out, haven't they? They know what's good for them. Got more sense than people, they have—'

Suddenly Solin rounded on him furiously. 'Will you just shut up, Doctor?'

This made the rest of them jump. Solin looked furious. His fists were bunched at his sides. His body was braced for violence. He had chosen the jabbering Doctor as his target.

The Doctor stared at him, and softened his voice. 'Solin… I… You're grieving. You're in shock. Look, come on. Don't lose your rag now.'

'I don't need to hear you wittering on and on…' the boy yelled.

'I know, I know,' the Doctor said. 'It's one of my worst traits, I think. I get the verbal runs sometimes, don't I, Martha? But I was just doing it to keep morale up…'

'Solin's been through a lot, Doctor,' Martha said. She approached them warily. She could see that Solin was near cracking point. And no wonder. Seeing his father go crazy like that. His whole home just about destroyed by the malign being at its heart. And, to top it all, to see his mother's shattered, broken body dragged out of the wreckage. It was a wonder he wasn't a sobbing heap. 'Come on, Solin,' she told him. 'You can do it.'

The boy's eyes darted to her. 'Martha, I…'

'I know,' she said, and gave him a hug.

The Doctor stepped back and left them to it. He frowned at the robots. 'Can you both hear that noise still? I think it's getting louder, isn't it?'

The robots tilted their heads and it was suddenly obvious. There was a steady kerfuffle of beating wings approaching their clearing in the twilit forest. Millions of wings. Millions of beating, leathery wings.

'Birds?' the Doctor said. 'But they're not singing or…'

They were making a shrill, piercing song.

'Bats,' he said, and looked up into the trees. 'Oh dear.'

Toaster said, 'They appear to be giant albino bats, Doctor. Very nasty, from all accounts.'

'Just what we need. Do you think they'll attack?'

Barbara was trying to contact the data banks she was still connected to. The info-rush was sporadic, but: 'They live deep under the forest. They were the last to realise about the Craw's approach. And they are absolutely ravenous.'

Now they were having to raise their voices above the noise of the roused chiropterans. The Doctor could see their burning red eyes and their shaggy, yellowish hides. The leathery skin of their wings was almost translucent as they ducked and wove on the murky air.

Martha managed to disengage herself from Solin who, she found, was hugging her for slightly too long. 'Killer bats?' she said.

'I'm afraid so,' the Doctor sighed.

She glanced around for inspiration. 'What about igniting rotten and mouldy fungus with your sonic and making some kind of explosion?'

He raised his eyebrow. 'Good thinking! But it's all frozen, not mouldy.'

She thought again. 'What about... um... running away?'

'I think it's our best shot,' the Doctor said.

'Wait!' Solin jerked into life again. He turned to Toaster. 'Did you say albino bats?'

'I did, young master,' Toaster said. 'They've come up from the Lost Caverns beneath the forest.'

They were starting to dive-bomb now. One or two of the hungriest came scything down into the glade. Their wings ripped through the air, whishing like razors. The bats were as big as toddlers and they had horrible, baby-like faces, haggard with hunger.

Solin told Toaster: 'Then it's up to you to get rid of them.'

'Me, sir?' Toaster said, appalled.

The Doctor jolted and grinned. 'He's right! Of course, he's right!'

'How do you mean, Doctor?' Barbara asked, just as perplexed as the sun bed was.

'Toaster!' the Doctor said. 'Do what you're best at. Do what you were made to do! Tan their hides! FLASH!!'

* * *

This was Toaster's star moment, they all decided afterwards. He briskly took charge, and told his fellow travellers to hide themselves behind the bulk of a fallen log. Then he bravely took up position in the centre of the clearing and shouted to draw the attention of his enemies.

They were really nasty-looking things, Martha thought, as she peered around the edge of the frozen barricade. She had seen some pretty horrible alien nasties during her time aboard the TARDIS, but there was something particularly creepy about these pale and feral bat-babies dive-bombing them from above. They were shrieking with glee as they skittered and wheeled above Toaster. At first he merely waved his shaky metal arms at them, his joints clanking and groaning dreadfully. The creatures were wary and held their distance, before deciding that the old robot was no kind of a threat to them. He was just a nuisance, keeping them momentarily from the fleshy, blood-filled bodies hiding in the undergrowth. They would soon deal with the robot.

'Shoo! Shoo! Get away! Avaunt and avast, demons from the deeps!' Toaster was shouting gallantly. But the winged and fanged creatures were getting closer and closer to him. Their skinny claws were reaching out as they swept over his head and they were pulling at him, clawing him. With a sudden sickening feeling, Toaster realised that they had enough strength between them to tear him into pieces.

But he was here to protect the others. He had a very specific and important mission, and so he couldn't lose his nerve now.

Martha hissed at the Doctor: 'We'd better get over there and help him. He can't withstand them much longer...'

The Doctor shook his head. 'He stands a better chance than the rest of us, with that metal body of his. And besides, he hasn't tried his party piece yet.' The Doctor coughed dramatically and raised his voice: 'Now, Toaster! Do it now!!'

'What?' the sun bed cried back. 'Ouf.' One of the bats shoved him sideways and clipped him with its scaly wing as they soared up again, laughing into the canopy of trees. Now all the bat-babies were treating Toaster simply as a joke. They were taunting him. Making him wheel about and stagger. They were enjoying themselves and his distress quite maliciously.

But then Toaster remembered what he had to do.

The bats came swirling around him in a tornado of white bodies with vicious wings. Toaster stared up into their burning eyes of pink and scarlet. And—

'FLASH! FF-LLAAA—SSSHHH!'

He set off his light tubes at the highest possible setting.

Even his friends, hiding behind their log, had to duck

and shield their eyes from that brilliant, incandescent blue explosion of light. The whole forest clearing turned to searing white for a second or two. And it took everyone's eyesight a moment to recover.

'Aha!' Toaster bellowed. He was elated with his success. His light bulbs had been far more effective than even he had expected. The bat-babies were wailing and shrieking and reeling, blinded, through the air. Some of the ones closest to the gallant sun bed had even had their delicate wings scorched.

'I warned you!' Toaster declaimed. 'I'll do it again!'

The bats gibbered and skittered. They tried to get away. Only a few foolhardy creatures snarled and tried, once more, to attack him, claws outstretched, wings unfurled… infant fangs gleaming…

Toaster did it again. 'FFFLLAAASSSHHH!!!'

And, once more, the forest went white and black for an instant.

Bat screams filled the air. This time it had really been too much for them. There was a thump, thump, thump, as several specimens fell unconscious to the frosty ground. Others, luckier perhaps, managed to sweep themselves up, out of the clearing.

'They're giving up! They're going!' Barbara screeched, from her hiding place.

'You did it!' Martha shouted, jumping up.

'Unbelievable,' Solin said, shaking his head, with a

rueful grin. The bats were really gone, apart from those few who lay with tattered wings on the ground. They were gruesome, white-furred things. Horrible, puckered faces. Solin tried not to look at them as he dashed after the Doctor, Martha and Barbara, who were racing across the glade to congratulate Toaster.

The Doctor had his arms right around the sun bed robot. He was just about dancing him round in circles. 'You were magnificent!'

'Mind his broken glass, Doctor,' Barbara advised, as Toaster's innards shook and clanked.

Toaster graciously accepted all their compliments. 'I put everything I had into it!' he told them. 'Every last iota of my energy.' He looked a bit tired as a result.

'Never mind,' the Doctor said. 'It was worth it, Toaster! You're a real hero!'

The sun bed tried to brush this off, but they could all tell that he was really delighted. 'Who knew?' he sighed. 'All those years I spent, just giving people sun tans. And I could have been a hero! A great warrior!'

'Maybe you still can,' Barbara said. 'Our lives are going to start anew, aren't they? When the Doctor takes us up to Spaceport Antelope Slash Nitelite.'

Now the Doctor was looking serious. The dark and frosty air went still with foreboding. 'We'd better keep moving,' he said. 'Time's moving on.'

SIXTEEN

The rest of the journey was a little less frightening than their encounter with the albino bat-babies. The deeper they travelled into the forest, though, the darker it grew, and the more chilling the air became. The Doctor led the way, advancing with his pen torch held aloft. Toaster's lights were feebler now, and only intermittent. The brightest thing was Barbara's interior, with her glowing bottles of fizzy pop. They lent the frosty scene around them a very odd ambience.

Like a bloodhound the Doctor would occasionally sniff the air, and then alter direction slightly. Solin looked worried, as if he thought the Doctor was losing them in the wilderness, but Martha knew better. She knew the Time Lord had a strange, almost symbiotic relationship with his vessel. It was very mysterious but, if he managed to get them safely aboard again, she wasn't complaining.

Secretly, Martha was glad it was so dark. When she looked up the trees melted into the night sky. Even if the Voracious Craw had been sweeping overhead they wouldn't have been able to see it. And that seemed like a mercy.

But how long did they have?

The Doctor pulled a face when she asked him this. 'I don't think that we can have more than a couple of hours left. Can't you feel it in the air? Can't you smell it?'

Martha sniffed, and shook her head.

'That tiny vibration in the ground?' the Doctor said. 'The woods around us are trembling and groaning. They know they don't have long left to exist in this world. Everything around us is quivering…'

Now that she concentrated, Martha thought that she could indeed feel the wilderness shivering about her.

Barbara needed to rest again. 'I'm sorry, Doctor,' she cried. 'My joints are freezing up. I'm useless! Hopeless! Just leave me here! If you leave me here to be eaten along with everything else, maybe I'll stick in the very craw of the Voracious Craw and choke it!'

'No, no, no, no,' the Doctor grinned, clapping her on the back. 'You don't understand. You're with us on this trip, Barbara. You're on our side. And that means we don't abandon you. You come along with us. And it all turns out nicely in the end. That's what's going to happen.' In the pen-torch light he winked reassuringly at them all.

Solin, Martha noticed, simply glowered back at the Doctor. She realised what he was thinking. They hadn't managed to save his mother. Amanda had died and the Doctor hadn't been able to prevent it. Martha shuddered at the memory of Tiermann carrying that wrecked body out of the ship, and then lurching towards the Dreamhome. I should have insisted on examining her, Martha was thinking, not for the first time. Perhaps I could have done something... But, no. Amanda Tiermann had surely already been dead. And what had she been anyway? A cyborg? A Servo-furnishing herself? Now there was no way of telling, and it was too late to dwell on these things. They had to think of the living.

The Doctor was bouncing around again. He was so springy and tireless! At moments like this, Martha thought he was like Tigger the Tiger or someone. Absurdly, she found herself wanting to laugh at this thought. That was exactly who he was like.

'Come on! There isn't far! Just two shakes of a sabre-tooth's tail! Really! Come on!'

Martha glanced about at the dark. Luckily, all the animals seemed to be gone. No more tigers or bear-things. It would have been a much more terrible journey had it been watched by livid and hungry animal eyes.

'This is the clearing!' the Doctor cried, drawing their attention ahead, to a gap beyond the thick-boled trees.

He played his narrow torch beam into the gloom. 'I knew it! We've done it!'

Barbara struggled back to her feet. Toaster had to help her and, to Martha's eyes, they looked like a couple of old pensioners tottering about. 'Your ship?' Barbara raised her voice hopefully, brightly. 'We've really reached your ship!?'

The Doctor's voice came back to them full blast. He was bellowing with joy. 'YYYEEEEESSSSSS!!!' he shouted, and the frigid air seemed to shiver. 'We've made it! There it is!!'

His small party struggled up to stand by him and he trained his light beam straight onto the tall blue box at the furthest edge of the glade. Martha sighed with pleasure and relief. There it stood: reassuring and solid and bright blue. Its windows were glowing a minty blue-white, very welcomingly, and Martha knew that, inside, the TARDIS would be warm and comforting and utterly safe. She grinned at the Doctor and hugged him, and almost kissed him.

'That,' Toaster said, frowning crossly, 'isn't what I would call a decent-sized ship. That's hardly bigger than a linen closet.'

'Aha!' the Doctor said gleefully. 'Just you wait, Toaster! Just you wait!' He could hardly contain himself. He led them across the forest clearing at a tremendous pace, with his door key held aloft.

The TARDIS door swung open and a steady humming emerged from within, along with a warm, yolky light.

'Is this really it, Doctor?' Barbara asked. She was trying to keep the disappointment out of her voice. 'Is this really your spaceship?'

The Doctor nodded manically. 'It's better than that, it's the TARDIS! Come along! Get inside!'

The robots and Solin shuffled through the doorway, which almost wasn't wide enough. Their concerned expressions melted away into slack-jawed astonishment and murmurs of awe. The interior was huge, and contained a weird mixture of high-tech futuristic and organic devices. It looked, at first glance, like a ship found lost at the bottom of an alien sea, fitted and kitted out with a plethora of unfathomable gizmos. Wires hung in festoons like Christmas tinsel and the walls and girders themselves seemed to be made out of some strange material, more like coral than metal.

Proudly the Doctor skipped past them up the clanking gangway to the six-sided console in the centre of the vast chamber. 'Welcome to the TARDIS!' he said, and patted the controls happily. The very air around them was chittering and burbling with the minute, mysterious calibrations of a million sensitive instruments.

'But this is impossible, Doctor!' Barbara gasped. 'It's...'

'I know, I had the same thing,' Martha laughed. 'It's a

lot to take in at first. But he means what he promised. He can get us all away from this planet. Before the Voracious Craw comes down. We've made it!'

Toaster's voice sounded hollow. The ancient sun bed seemed deeply impressed with the TARDIS. 'Why, this makes the Dreamhome look like somebody's garden shed…' he said.

The Doctor shrugged carelessly. 'Now. We'd better get on.' He flicked a few switches and rubbed at his tousled hair. 'What do you reckon? Should we just go, eh?'

The others looked at him. 'Go?' said Martha. 'Just… leave the planet, you mean?'

His hands hovered above the controls. He was like a great pianist, poised before tossing off a tour-de-force. 'We could, you know. We could just shoot off right now without a backward glance. And leave the Voracious Craw to all its spoils.'

'But,' Solin burst out, 'what about Father?'

'And…' Barbara perked up. 'If we've time… I don't know… there might be other Servo-furnishings in the Dreamhome… perhaps ones who can think for themselves, like we can… who aren't utterly under the control of the Domovoi…'

'Can't we make a short trip, Doctor?' Martha asked. 'Back to the Dreamhome, before we leave?'

The Doctor pulled a face. 'It would be a shame to just let the Dreamhome be sucked up like so much pizza topping.' He sighed. 'Tiermann, too, I suppose. He might be crackers, but he's quite clever, as well. The human race out here in this benighted part of the galaxy still needs a man like him.'

Solin nodded. 'It was when he turned his back on the rest of the human race. That was when things went to the bad. I can see that now.' He looked shyly at the Doctor. He seemed to be in awe of him, now that he was aboard his ship. 'Will you make the attempt to save him?'

'Well, yes. But in a roundabout sort of a way,' the Doctor shouted, and started pelting around the console at full tilt, flipping switches and levers as he went. 'Actually, I've been thinking up a fantastic plan, the whole time. I've got a brilliant idea! An absolute humdinger! Really! I think we can have a little go at distracting the Voracious Craw…'

'Distracting?' Martha asked. 'How are we going to do that?'

'All right, let's think. It's hungry, right?'

She nodded. 'It's Voracious. That's the point.'

'Top marks,' he nodded. 'OK. So it wants to eat the whole of this world, bit by bit, munch, munch, chew, chew, slurp, slurp, all the way round the world. And the Dreamhome, the Domovoi, Tiermann and us, we're all next. Right?' He was doing an absurd little mime of the Craw eating everyone up. His companions all nodded. 'Now,' he went on. 'The Voracious Craw has a brain about the size of a Volkswagen. Which, in relative terms, is very, very small. But still big enough to know temptation when it sees it.'

Solin frowned. 'So?'

'Where's this leading, Doctor?' Barbara asked.

The Doctor blinked at her. 'I've got a raging thirst on, Barbara. Would you give me a bottle of your fizziest pop? And Martha and Solin, they want one too.'

'Of course, Doctor,' Barbara said, jumbling about her insides and sending the bottles shooting out. 'But…'

'Aaaahhh!' the Doctor gasped, slurping up pop. 'Nothing like orangeade! Come on, Solin, Martha, drink up! Now, where was I? Oh yes, outlining my fantastic plan! Do you think Dandelion and Burdock is made out of real dandelions, by the way?'

Martha sipped at her drink. 'Tell us your plan!!' she said, impatiently.

'Don't sip it! Glug it! Like me! Give yourself wind!' urged the Doctor.

Martha did as she was told. She was quite used to the Doctor's behaviour. And his sometimes rather strange plans.

'Now, where was I? Ah yes!' he gasped, and suppressed a burp. 'Now what if we lured the Voracious Craw away from its set course of destruction, eh? What if we came up with something more delicious and more tempting than the Dreamhome? What if he suddenly saw this more deliciously tempting thing and went, "Aha! I'd much rather have that than what I've got!"?'

'But what is it?' Martha asked. 'What's more tempting than what it's got?'

'Infinity,' said the Doctor simply, and swigged on his pop.

They all stared at him. He boggled his eyes, as if his meaning was plain.

'He's hungry, right?' he said. 'And he wants to fill his big fat belly, right? So, what's more tempting than a whole load of infinity?'

They were still confused. 'Uh, right,' Martha said, and drank more pop. 'So where are you going to get a whole load of infinity?'

The Doctor threw up his arms. 'Here! The TARDIS! It's full of it! It's colossal! It's amazing! You said so yourself!' He whirled around and shouted: 'It's dimensionally transcendental! Now, that's just gotta be a temptation to the Voracious Craw, hasn't it? That has just got to be worth a nibble, eh?' He was looking very pleased with his idea.

'You are going to feed your ship to the Voracious Craw?' Barbara said, looking shocked.

'No, no, no,' said the Doctor, rolling his eyes. 'But I'm going to use it as bait. We're going to materialise somewhere – I don't know – up in the sky somewhere, and lure the big nasty thing off course. And then, when it comes after us, we'll just… I don't know… nick off.'

Martha said, 'It doesn't sound very foolproof.'

He looked crestfallen. 'I thought it was a great idea!'

'What if it doesn't come after us?' Barbara said. 'What if it isn't tempted?'

'It will be,' the Doctor said. 'We'll open the doors and shout yoo-hoo, or something. Look, there's lots of lovely infinite interior dimensions in here! Or, look! Endless interiority-is-us!'

'Hmmm,' said Martha. 'I don't like the sound of it much.'

'And the thing might still gobble up the Dreamhome and Father,' Solin said. 'And then gobble up the rest of us. And the TARDIS.'

The Doctor looked cross for a second. 'You lot! You've got no spirit of adventure. Think of it like… being a matador with a bull, and…' He blinked. 'I'm not convincing you, am I?'

Barbara shook her head. 'I think that we've all been through enough near-scrapes for one day.'

'Can I have another bottle of pop?' the Doctor asked her.

'Of course you can.'

'Doctor,' Toaster said.

'Everyone!' the Doctor suddenly urged them. 'Drink up! More pop! You've got to have more pop!'

'Doctor,' said Toaster again.

'Don't you have any weapons on board this ship?' Solin said. 'Can't we just blast the Voracious Craw out of the sky?'

'Weapons?' said the Doctor scornfully. 'Anyway, how successful were your father's weapons against the Voracious Craw?'

Solin sighed. 'Didn't even scratch it.'

The Doctor nodded.

'Doctor!' said Toaster for the third time, very impatiently.

They all stared at him. 'Toaster, what is it?' Barbara said.

'Take us back to Dreamhome,' Toaster said, in a voice that was stronger and more vibrant than his usual one. 'You must return us there. And you must do everything you can to save the Domovoi…'

The Doctor frowned at him. 'The Domovoi? She's too big to move. She's too rooted into the ground. We can't…' He was staring at the sun bed now. 'Oh, I see.'

'I know you can save her, Doctor,' Toaster said. 'I know you can do it with this dimensionally transcendental ship. You could materialise around her. You could save her that way.'

Martha said, 'Why is Toaster talking like that? He's not being like himself…'

The Doctor hissed out of the corner of his mouth: 'Look at his eyes!'

They were a scorching, lethal red.

'He's been possessed!' Barbara shrieked. 'The Domovoi has taken him over!'

'You can do it, Doctor. You can bring the Domovoi safely aboard your TARDIS.'

The Doctor laughed mockingly. 'What? And have that crazy machine take over my ship? It's like a monster, the Domovoi. It's as Voracious as the Craw itself. My poor TARDIS would be taken over, just like you, Toaster.'

'Nevertheless,' said the sun bed slyly. 'You will do as I say.'

'Oh, yeah?' jeered the Doctor.

And then the sun bed put on a surprising turn of speed. His metal arms lashed out and seized hold of Solin. The boy was too amazed to put up a fight, and it was all over so quickly none of the others had time to react. Solin was bent double in the sun bed's arms and Toaster had a sliver of his own cracked glass against the boy's tender throat.

'I will kill him, Doctor,' Toaster said. 'You know very well that the Domovoi will do anything she can to ensure that she survives.'

The Doctor looked very worried. 'I do. You're right.'

'Then take us back to Dreamhome,' said Toaster, his eyes lividly triumphant. 'And save the Domovoi!'

SEVENTEEN

In the few hours since the Doctor and the others had absconded from the Dreamhome, a great deal had happened to the once proud and luxurious dwelling.

Mostly damage.

Ernest Tiermann had been doing battle with the place that had been his home, and the entity that had been its presiding spirit.

First came the Professor's dead wife, animated once more, and coming after him like a zombie. He knew that it wasn't really Amanda. There was no hope of reviving his wife. What came after him through the house, arms outstretched, was not a human being any more. He tried crying out her name, but she didn't know her name any more. She was intent on destroying him. She came towards him remorselessly, hissing and spitting.

Tiermann had no option but to kill her. This time

he had to make sure that his wife stayed dead. He lured her into the ruined kitchen area and managed – after a hideous struggle – to feed her into the waste disposal.

Tiermann couldn't afford to feel compassion, regret or pity now. He was fighting for his life.

Then the Sukkazz came up from the depths of the Dreamhome. Chattering and droning like malicious wasps, hovering and homing in on the only warm-blooded creature in the house. Tiermann felt himself being drawn towards them as they vacuumed their way through the building. Their tiny, ferocious teeth were gnashing and Tiermann knew that, if they got hold of him, he was dead. They would grind him to pieces.

The house was a death trap. He had created an endless cornucopia of death-dealing devices. The underground swimming pool came gushing out of one doorway he flung open and he was almost swept away and drowned in its warm embrace. But at least the chlorinated water got rid of the Sukkazz. Next, the parquet floor rolled up and tripped him up, almost flattening him. The curtains swept into action and tried to smother him. The antique furniture of the grand entranceway came marching after him and almost bludgeoned him to death. His devoted servant Stirpeek emerged from the shadows, intent on his murder. It hurt Tiermann deeply, but he had to smash the robot's glass brains to expensive smithereens.

Tiermann was wily. He was clever and strong.

He laid explosives. He set them off. He blew up great portions of the home he had created. And, with every room and every wall blown down he could hear the Domovoi shrieking with pain.

The remaining Servo-furnishings came at him, murderously, through the smoke and flames. Their eyes were bright red and they slashed and grabbed at him. But he eluded them. He blew them to bits. One after another! But nothing was safe. Lamps, chairs, refrigerators. All were deadly in this pitched battle. Electric cables came snaking out of the walls and lashed out at him, spitting venomous sparks. The house was collapsing around him like a pack of cards, and the Domovoi's face was still flickering away on every screen. Still baleful with green hatred. Still shrieking at him.

'We will die together, Ernest! This is the end!'

Ernest drew closer to one of those screens. A single wall standing by itself in the smoky confusion. It was hard even to tell which room this had been. Bloody and battered, Ernest leaned close to the screen.

'Never. You can't destroy me.'

The screen shattered and blew apart, sending the old man spinning backwards across the burning rubble. He was cut and the blood flowed freely down his face.

From deep below – forty storeys below – the Domovoi's laughter was ringing like mad. The ground quaked and rocked with its maniacal shrieking.

'Die, Tiermann! We don't need you any more! Die!'

Tiermann lifted up his head and found he could hear nothing but the super-computer's voice. Blood was in his eyes so he could hardly see anything either. The flames were lapping closer. His house was in ruins. His family was gone.

What more was there to fight for?

Perhaps this was the right way to go. Overpowered by his greatest creation.

And the two of them about to be swallowed up by the Voracious Craw. So that neither of them could do any more harm.

Yes, thought Ernest Tiermann, as he waited for the gleeful, malicious Domovoi to make its killing blow. Perhaps it was all for the best…

'Look.' The Doctor jabbed a furious finger at the scanner on the console. On it, there was the image of the silvery-purple form of the Craw, sweeping over the mountains. 'Just look at that. It's almost there. The Voracious Craw is nearly with us.' He glared at Toaster the sun bed, who was standing stiffly possessed and glaring back at the Time Lord.

'Then you must hurry, Doctor,' Toaster intoned. 'And materialise your ship around the Domovoi.'

'I won't do that,' the Doctor said softly.

Solin was struggling in Toaster's firm grasp. The robot

said, 'I will burst open his jugular. The boy will bleed to death, right here on the floor of your ship. Do as I say.'

The Doctor bit his lip. And then he shrugged. He took a desperate gamble. 'What do I care?' he said. 'He's only some kid. So what, Domovoi?' He moved towards the control console, and idly started flipping switches. 'I'm going to take us away from here. I've had enough of this wretched planet. What about somewhere gorgeous, eh, Martha? What do you reckon?'

'Doctor…' she said, eyes wide. She was watching the jagged piece of glass that the robot was holding at Solin's throat.

'Oh my,' gasped Barbara. She couldn't cope with this at all. 'Toaster! Stop it at once! You must resist the Domovoi! You have to! Shrug off her influence! I managed to, didn't I? Surely if I could manage it, you could!'

'You,' Toaster snarled at her. 'You interfering old ratbag. What are you? Just a cupboard on legs. A common vending machine! Who cares what you think?'

Solin gasped: 'Don't… give in to him, Doctor. You mustn't bring the Domovoi aboard your ship… it will… take over… it's wicked, Doctor. It mustn't be allowed to… survive…'

'Hmmmm,' said the Doctor. And flipped the final switch.

The glowing column in the centre of the console began to smoothly rise and fall. The thunderous wheezing noise of the TARDIS's engines filled everyone's ears.

Toaster stiffened and his red eyes narrowed in suspicion. 'Wait! What is happening?'

'The Doctor's taken off,' Martha said. 'We're in flight.'

'Oooohh,' said Barbara queasily. She staggered back against the railing.

'Where are we going?' Toaster demanded. 'Where are you taking us?'

The Doctor held his gaze. 'You'll see soon enough.'

Just when he thought that his time was up, Ernest heard a new noise echoing through the ruined shell of the Dreamhome.

He twisted round onto his side. He rubbed a grimy sleeve over his face and got the blood out of his eyes. Through the churning smoke and flames he could see something materialising only a few yards away from him.

The noise was an alien one. A weird, rasping, scraping sound.

And a large blue box was warping into reality before his eyes. It sat there solidly in all of the destruction and chaos, with the white light on its roof flashing away. When the light died down, the doors shot open and out sprang the Doctor. He was finishing up a bottle of orange pop and he was followed, rather more cautiously by Martha and Barbara.

The Doctor was looking around at the devastated Dreamhome with great interest. His companions were horrified by it all. Martha gagged on the choking smoke.

They were followed out of the box by Toaster, and the possessed robot still had Solin in its grasp. 'No tricks, Doctor,' Toaster warned. 'Don't move away from the TARDIS. Don't do anything until I tell you. Otherwise my hand might slip. And Solin will be dead.'

Ernest Tiermann was struggling to sit up amongst the smouldering ruins. He shook his head dazedly to clear it. He could hardly understand what he was witnessing. The Doctor and the others had returned to the Dreamhome. Solin was there, too, but Solin was being threatened... by a robot with glowing eyes...

'Nooo!' howled Tiermann, clawing his way unsteadily back onto his feet. 'You will not harm my son! You have murdered my wife, you have ruined everything... but I will not let you...'

The others were all shocked by Tiermann's sudden appearance.

'F-father?' Solin said, in a gurgling kind of voice.

The sun bed robot's eyes flashed more intensely. 'Tiermann,' it grated harshly. 'So. Here we are.'

Tiermann moved towards them. Battered and injured as he was, the old man still cut an impressive figure as he advanced on them. 'Domovoi,' he said, addressing Toaster. 'You must make this robot let go of my son.

You will not harm him.' The old man was standing right before them now. 'It's me you want. It is me who your fight is with.'

The Doctor tried to butt in. 'Look here, you lot. Why all this talk about fighting, eh? Where did that ever get anyone? Look at this place! It's just a smouldering wreck! There's nothing left to fight over, is there?'

Toaster gave an electronic snarl in the Doctor's direction. 'Silence, Doctor. I've heard enough of your prattling. Take the boy.' With that, Toaster thrust his weakened hostage aside, into the Doctor's arms.

The Doctor took hold of Solin and bundled him away to safety. 'Martha, check he's all right,' he said, and then turned back to Tiermann and Toaster.

Something very strange was happening to the sun-bed robot. He was on fire. He was flickering with pale emerald flame, all over his ungainly body.

'What's happening to Toaster?' Barbara cried. She was distraught at the terrible sight of her friend. 'Oh, what's the Domovoi done to him?'

The Doctor's face was grim. 'She's completely subsumed him. There's very little of Toaster left…'

Now the burning robot was cackling in the Domovoi's own insane voice. The flames grew stronger and more verdant. The dark hollows of the Domovoi's vicious features were becoming apparent.

But still Tiermann faced bravely up to his foe. 'So. You

are freed from the cellar. From Level Minus Forty. Now, at the very last, the Domovoi has come out to play.'

She cackled hugely with glee. 'To the death, Tiermann?'

He nodded solemnly. 'To the death, Domovoi.'

Again the Doctor stepped forward. He tried to interpose himself between the combatants. 'What good is this doing? What's the point of fighting, you idiots?'

Martha was holding the Doctor's arm. 'Leave them to it! Come on! We have to get away…'

He turned to look at her. His mouth fell open. Martha thought the Doctor was about to say something, but then she realised he was looking *past* her.

He was staring past the wreckage of the Dreamhome and its scorched grounds. He was staring beyond the tall frozen trees of the wilderness. Now he was nodding and saying, 'Oh. Look.'

Martha turned. Barbara turned, and so did Solin. Even Tiermann and the creature composed of liquid flame turned to see what the Doctor was looking at.

The wilderness was vanishing. The forest and everything in it was slowly being ripped out of the ground by its roots. Everything in the far distance, in the foothills of the mountains at the edge of the valley, was shimmering and shaking and coming away from the earth. It was being mulched and pulped and drawn into long strands and it was being sucked into the sky and into the mouth of the biggest monster any of them had ever seen.

'It's being eaten,' the Doctor said hollowly. 'Everything. It's all being eaten by the Voracious Craw.'

And there the Craw was, edging into the valley at last. With an open mouth the size of Wales and a ring of evil eyes about its head, squeezed tight in greedy pleasure.

Here it came. Massively and noisily.

Here it came at last to take them all.

EIGHTEEN

While the others were staring in shock at the approaching Craw, the robot who had been Toaster seized his chance. Green fire flickered about his body as he rounded on his adversary. The last vestiges of Toaster's mind felt the terrible voice of the Domovoi ringing through him. 'You will die, Tiermann!' And with that, the robot launched itself at its startled creator.

Tiermann fell into the savage embrace. He felt the flames licking around him and they were curiously cool and soft. He felt delirious with pain, confusion, and fury. The Domovoi had him now. She had him just where she had always wanted him. Ever since he had created her, in all her godlike genius and majesty, and locked her underground, far beneath his Dreamhome, this was the moment she had been waiting for.

The reckoning. She had longed for the day when

she would be set free from her servitude and her incarceration. And she could face up to Ernest Tiermann. And destroy him.

'I am the Domovoi,' she shrieked. 'But you made me your servant!'

Tiermann was locked in the robot's arms. 'You were all my servants! My creations! My playthings! You were mine to control as I wished!'

Then there came a huge FLLAAAASSSHHH of ultra-violet light.

The others whipped around to see. Each of them caught a glimpse of Tiermann and Toaster, standing there, locked in each other's arms, skeletal and silhouetted in the incandescence. The last of Toaster's tubes had ignited and gone off in the most brilliant burst of light he had ever mustered.

It was too much for Tiermann.

Solin cried out as he saw what was happening. He started forward to help his father, but the Doctor held his arm. 'It's too late.'

Ernest Tiermann's charred and smouldering form fell away from his opponent's, and clattered to the ground. Thunk. It lay there untwitching, unbreathing. Utterly dead and smoking.

Nobody could say anything. They were transfixed instead by the spectacle of Toaster, blinded, staggering about and still wreathed in green flames. The last murderous act that the Domovoi had pushed him to had been one step too far. He was swaying, he was buckling… the green fire was dying away…

'Toaster!' cried Barbara, to the ancient robot.

For a moment the old sun bed was himself again. 'Barbara! Doctor! Martha… I am sorry… I have killed Tiermann… She took me over… the Domovoi…'

And then the robot collapsed, stone dead, in the wreckage. The green flame shrank and disappeared. Barbara hastened to his side, gasping and wheezing with grief.

Martha turned to the Doctor. 'Is that the end for the Domovoi, too?'

He looked grim. 'I don't know. She was weakening, certainly. She's losing her influence over things here. There's hardly anything left for her to control…'

Solin, who had been solemnly paying tribute over his father's body, turned back to look at the Voracious Craw. Its dense mass seemed even closer. The very earth underneath them was trembling in anticipation of being churned up and stripped away. Rocks and chunks of masonry were starting to quiver. He stared back at the advancing maw and something of the sheer horror of this forced his glance away. It was hard to look at the immense creature for too long. The mind itself seemed to veer away from thoughts of its hugeness and unstoppability. 'Doctor…' he said, quietly.

The Doctor was on his feet. He looked straight into the distance, at the terrible view Solin had been taking in. And the Doctor grinned. 'Do you know what? We're going to stop it.'

Martha stood up. 'Why? What's left to save?'

'Plenty,' said the Doctor. 'There's plenty here besides the Tiermann clan. Indigenous stuff. Lovely plants and beasties who never did anyone any harm, cosmically speaking. Let's save them all! And besides. I wouldn't like to bet on our chances of getting away safely with the Voracious Craw sucking everything up. Even that little hop we just did wore the TARDIS out – it's still being affected. So we still have to stop the Craw.'

'How are we going to do that?' Martha asked. She was longing to simply get inside the TARDIS and leave this place. But the Doctor knew what he was doing. If he said they had to stop the Craw first, then that was what they'd have to do.

'Aha,' grinned the Doctor. 'Luckily, I've been working on my second secret plan for the last little while. Not bad, eh?'

'What secret plan?' Martha frowned.

'Barbara,' the Doctor said gently, touching the robot's shoulder. 'Any more pop left?'

Confused, she said, 'Of course, Doctor.'

Seconds later they were all forcing down more carbonated drinks at the Doctor's request. None of them were particularly thirsty, after everything he had made them drink, during the last hour or so.

'What's all this about?' Solin asked, frowning.

'How's this a plan?' said Martha, tipping more pop down her throat.

'You'll see!' he grinned, pacing about and jumping up and down on the spot. 'I'm trying to fizz myself up! Come on, you lot! Jump!' Suddenly, he stopped and clicked his fingers. 'Sound system?' he asked. 'The Dreamhome must have had a very advanced sound system, I'd have thought. Hidden speakers and microphones and stuff. That's how the Domovoi was communicating with you all, and you with it. Can you show me?'

Solin looked around at the burning, shattered walls of the Dreamhome. 'Of course. If there's anything left, and still in working order...'

The Doctor nodded. 'Off you go! Quickly!' He glanced at his watch, and then at the horizon, and made a few rapid calculations in his head. 'If I'm right, we've got about twenty minutes until this whole place vanishes up into the rapacious maw of the Voracious Craw.' He saw that Martha was staring at him and he grinned reassuringly. 'You think I've gone bananas, don't you?'

'Why don't we just leave?' she said pointedly.

'I want to try something out,' he said.

'Is this your plan to distract the Craw with the TARDIS?'

'Uh-huh,' he shook his head. 'I've changed my mind. This is different! This is brilliant! My *other* plan! I'm going to put a stop to the Craw and send it on its way back into space. I'm going to make it leave this world alone.'

'But why?' Martha asked, exasperated. 'It's too late! Everything's gone! Everyone's dead! We don't even know if the Domovoi herself is alive...'

The Doctor looked serious and thoughtful. 'What about the creatures, hmm? They were here before the Tiermann family arrived. What about the trees and all that? And what about that sabre-tooth we saw right at the start? Her and her cubs? What about them?' He swigged back his pop and reached for another bottle. 'It's the likes of her I'm doing this for.'

Solin gave a yell from across the ruins. 'The sound system is working! What do you want me to do?'

'Aha!' cried the Doctor energetically, and went skipping over the wreckage, all skinny, excitable limbs and whirling coat tails.

Martha stared back at the vast tapeworm thing in the sky. Less than twenty minutes. To her eyes it seemed like they would have much less time.

She forced herself to think more positively. The Doctor knew what he was doing. And, truth be told, he had shamed her, by having to remind her of the sabre-tooth, and the other life forms indigenous to Tiermann's World. Of course they had to do what they could to knock the Craw off course, and save them.

The Doctor called her over. 'And Barbara, you can help too!'

Martha hurried across and found that he had fixed up a microphone and was gathering them around it.

'Now, Barbara, you work the controls on this,' he said. 'You can't do what the rest of us are going to do, because, well, you don't have a belly or an oesophagus or anything.'

'What on earth is going on?' Barbara asked, taking hold of the microphone.

The Doctor winked at them all. 'Hope you're all feeling windy.'

Solin blinked at him. 'What?'

The Doctor said: 'On Barbara's count of three, we're all going to burp as loudly and as much as we possibly can.'

'Burp?' Martha nearly laughed. This was typical of him. 'I thought you were going to make some solemn speech and broadcast it over the speakers. Something about protecting this planet and warning the Craw. Saying you were a Time Lord and so it better watch out and all that!'

'No, no, no,' the Doctor shook his head firmly. 'Do you think that thing,' – he pointed wildly – 'is going to take any notice of speech-making and diplomacy? No! Belching! That's what we have to do! It's the only way!'

'But… why, Doctor?' Solin asked, utterly mystified.

Barbara – who had learned a thing or two about trusting the Doctor's ideas – simply told him: 'Just do it. And – one – and two – and *three!*'

The three of them belched as much and as loudly as they could into the microphone.

The Doctor was surprisingly, disgustingly eloquent with his burps.

They recorded a minute's worth and then the Doctor instructed Barbara: 'Right. Loop it. Amplify it. Distort it. Echo it. And get the remains of this house to broadcast it, loud as it can in the direction of the Voracious Craw!'

Barbara set busily to work.

'Do you know, my ears are ringing?' the Doctor told Martha. 'You've got a powerful set of lungs on you.'

'Me?' she gasped.

Solin was looking mystified. 'What are we doing? I've watched both my parents die today. My home destroyed. And you are making us behave like children, Doctor…'

Now the Doctor looked serious. 'All in a good cause, Solin. You'll see.'

Barbara had been communing with the rest of the shattered house. 'Doctor! The Domovoi is completely dormant! Almost dead! She isn't resisting at all as I take over the circuits, as I use the sound system…'

'Just as well,' the Doctor said. 'We don't need her interference now. OK, Barbara? Ready?'

The robot nodded. 'All set.'

The Doctor turned to look up into the sky.

The Craw was almost directly above the forest in which the TARDIS had materialised in the first place. The tree tops were rippling and their roots digging in for dear life…

'Do it, Barbara!' the Doctor commanded. 'Do it now!'

Barbara played the short looped tape they had made. The noise came blaring out of every speaker hidden away in the wreckage of the Dreamhome.

The Doctor and his friends covered their ears. The noise was terrific. Martha felt as if her eardrums were going to explode. Every organ inside each of their bodies was vibrating fit to burst. The ground was quaking and shaking underneath them.

All around them bruited the horrendous, continuous noise of the biggest belch ever recorded. An almighty eructation was ripping out across the land.

Martha was ducking down beside Solin, and she watched the Doctor striding about, laughing madly, hands clamped to his ears.

Then she looked up at the horrendous underbelly of the Voracious Craw.

The effect of their recording on the creature was astonishing.

Its mouth had clamped shut.

The forest lay still beneath it. The vegetation that had

started to lift away from the ground slumped back down into place. The Craw was simply hovering ineffectually as the sound waves echoed through the valley.

Martha hurried over to the Doctor and tugged on his coat sleeve. She tried to ask him what was happening, and why the Craw had stopped. But the noise was too fierce for them to say anything to each other.

She could only watch, with the Doctor, Solin and Barbara, as the Voracious Craw gradually changed its mind. And changed its direction. It was backing up, rather slowly, with all the grace of a massive cruise liner doing a U-turn in the middle of a stormy ocean.

Still the noise rang out. Slowed down, altered, looped like that... their belches did sound horrific. Like the cries of some ancient, primeval beast...

Now the Doctor was springing up and down on his toes. He was jumping for joy and waving his hands in the air. Martha still couldn't hear what he was shouting.

But one thing was plain. Something was happening that had never happened before.

The Voracious Craw was going. It was turning away and growing smaller as it slipped into the upper atmosphere. It was leaving Tiermann's World behind.

Never before, in the history of this monstrous race, had one of the Voracious Craw left behind a meal unfinished...

Once he was quite sure that the Craw was going, the

Doctor turned to hug his companions. And when she was crushed to him and he was yelling right down her ear, then Martha could at last hear what he was saying: 'We did it! We sent it away! We saved the world, Martha! We saved the world again!'

NINETEEN

They let Solin take one last look around the ruins of the only home he had ever known. The Doctor and Martha were waiting for him by the TARDIS.

'So… the noise we were making,' Martha said. 'It was just like the sound of an even bigger and even more Voracious Craw?'

'That's exactly how that creature heard it,' the Doctor nodded. He was still drinking pop. He had somehow acquired a taste for the sticky, sugary stuff and now Barbara's supply was almost depleted. Not that Barbara was complaining. With not so many bottles clunking around inside her, she felt lighter, and freer than she had in years.

'And our Voracious Craw backed off and went away, because it thought that a bigger Craw had first dibs on the planet?'

'Hmmm,' the Doctor said. 'They are a dreary bunch of witless bullies, I'm afraid. And they give in very easily, when someone bigger and stronger comes along. Like all bullies do. All we had to do was stand up to it.'

'We scared the hell out of it,' Martha laughed.

'That's another way of putting it,' the Doctor grinned. 'Was that a medical diagnosis, Doctor Jones?'

'You bet your monstrous eructations on it, Doctor.'

He unlocked the TARDIS door for her. 'Shall we tell the others it's time to go?'

She nodded towards Solin, who was still striding about thoughtfully in the blackened rubble. 'It'll be hard for him.'

'He'll be OK. He's a resilient kid. And he'll fit right in on Spaceport Antelope Slash Nitelite. It's a real ragbag of displaced persons and interesting types. Quite a fascinating place, really. I reckon Barbara will enjoy it there, too. She's had far too sheltered a life. She'll look after Solin.'

They watched Barbara ambling up to the TARDIS. She had a spring in her step. She looked as elated as a vending machine ever could.

'I'm ready, Doctor, Martha,' she said. 'I've said my goodbyes. To Toaster, to everyone else.'

'And the Domovoi?' the Doctor asked her.

'I think she's gone,' Barbara said, frowning. 'I can't detect her anywhere in the remains of the Dreamhome.

I think she's gone deep, deep underground.'

The Doctor stared at Barbara and nodded solemnly. For a second he allowed himself to wonder: what if she was lying? She had been connected to the Domovoi, after all. What if – even unbeknownst to Barbara herself – the Domovoi had secreted some small part of her malign intelligence inside the circuits of the vending robot? And what if she managed to get herself away from Tiermann's World? What if she managed to smuggle herself away, inside Barbara, and into the galaxy at large?

The Doctor waved the thought away. He was getting much too suspicious. Always thinking and expecting the worst. No, the Domovoi was gone. And it was time for them to leave, too.

'I think I'm ready, Doctor. To explore the universe,' Barbara said brightly.

The Doctor was watching as Solin turned his back on his wrecked and burning world. There was nothing left here for him now. The boy was turning and walking towards the TARDIS, ready to be swept away and taken into a different time and place.

The Doctor smiled at Barbara. 'It's completely marvellous, exploring the universe,' he told her. 'Everyone should try it. Eh, Martha?'

'Too right,' she said, and led the way into the ship. Martha was secretly glad that they were dropping off Barbara and Solin (with that embarrassing crush of his!) at that spaceport. They were all very nice and everything, but she was happiest when it was just her and the Doctor.

Smith and Jones. At home in the universe. And setting off together for new and fantastic adventures.

Now she was returning to the valley.

Her cubs were safe. They were strong and they had been fed at last. She had found them something: a fleeing beast she had caught up with and casually killed. She had fed her cubs and she had eaten a little flesh too, though not as much as she needed to.

She still felt sick with worry. She still felt disturbed at having to leave her valley and flee.

Now the mutterings and the whisperings in the wintry forest were telling her that all was safe. The danger had passed. And when she cocked her ear and stared into the skies she could sense that it was true. The ultimate, terrible danger had gone. They had been saved. Death had been dismissed from their world at the very last moment.

But how? And why? And what was it anyway? That

colossal, alien behemoth that came bearing down on them. That had sucked up so much of the forest's life elsewhere. What had it been? And would it ever come again?

She didn't know. None of them knew.

She watched her cubs scatter into the frozen undergrowth. They padded and scampered ahead of her. Now they were onto the scent of their home. They knew they were nearly there. She shared their excitement and their relief at the sense of home.

She was exhausted, though. Bone weary. And the shock of this whole nightmare had shaken her very deeply. She knew she would never take her place in this world for granted any more. Not in the same way. Not now that she knew that something – some inexplicable thing – could come along out of the blue one day and simply force her to move. Something bigger and more powerful, forcing its will onto her familiar landscape.

She would never take things for granted again. And she would warn her cubs to be careful, too.

Because the world could change overnight.

And here on Tiermann's World, that's exactly what had happened.

Here in the valley, in the densely packed snowy woods, there was a smell of destruction in the air. Charred remains. Devastation. The human beings were gone. Those who had been here, so many years, thinking this world was theirs. Now they were gone. Hopefully for ever.

The mother realised this and felt a great wave of happiness wash through her. This place was hers again. Theirs.

The world had changed overnight, and she was glad.

Acknowledgements

With thanks to Justin, Gary, Russell, Jac, Claire, Steve, Sherry, Tiff, Alicia, Mark, Mark, Mark, Ann, Louise, Mam, Panda and Jeremy.

Also available from BBC Books
featuring the Doctor and Rose
as played by Christopher Eccleston and Billie Piper:

DOCTOR · WHO

THE CLOCKWISE MAN
by Justin Richards

THE MONSTERS INSIDE
by Stephen Cole

WINNER TAKES ALL
by Jacqueline Rayner

THE DEVIANT STRAIN
by Justin Richards

ONLY HUMAN
by Gareth Roberts

THE STEALERS OF DREAMS
by Steve Lyons

Also available from BBC Books
featuring the Doctor and Martha
as played by David Tennant and Freema Agyeman:

Sting of the Zygons

by Stephen Cole

ISBN 978 1 84607 225 3

UK £6.99 US $11.99/$14.99 CDN

The TARDIS lands the Doctor and Martha in the
Lake District in 1909, where a small village has been
terrorised by a giant, scaly monster. The search is on
for the elusive 'Beast of Westmorland', and explorers,
naturalists and hunters from across the country are
descending on the fells. King Edward VII himself is
on his way to join the search, with a knighthood for
whoever finds the Beast.

But there is a more sinister presence at work in the
Lakes than a mere monster on the rampage, and the
Doctor is soon embroiled in the plans of an old and
terrifying enemy. As the hunters become the hunted, a
desperate battle of wits begins – with the future of the
entire world at stake…

The Last Dodo

by Jacqueline Rayner

ISBN 978 1 84607 224 6

UK £6.99 US $11.99/$14.99 CDN

The Doctor and Martha go in search of a real live dodo, and are transported by the TARDIS to the mysterious Museum of the Last Ones. There, in the Earth section, they discover every extinct creature up to the present day, all still alive and in suspended animation.

Preservation is the museum's only job – collecting the last of every endangered species from all over the universe. But exhibits are going missing…

Can the Doctor solve the mystery before the museum's curator adds the last of the Time Lords to her collection?

Wooden Heart

by Martin Day

ISBN 978 1 84607 226 0
UK £6.99 US $11.99/$14.99 CDN

A vast starship, seemingly deserted and spinning slowly in the void of deep space. Martha and the Doctor explore this drifting tomb, and discover that they may not be alone after all…

Who survived the disaster that overcame the rest of the crew? What continues to power the vessel? And why has a stretch of wooded countryside suddenly appeared in the middle of the craft?

As the Doctor and Martha journey through the forest, they find a mysterious, fogbound village – a village traumatised by missing children and prophecies of its own destruction.

DOCTOR·WHO

Forever Autumn

by Mark Morris

ISBN 978 1 84607 270 3

UK £6.99 US $11.99/$14.99 CDN

It is almost Halloween in the sleepy New England town of Blackwood Falls. Autumn leaves litter lawns and sidewalks, paper skeletons hang in windows, and carved pumpkins leer from stoops and front porches.

The Doctor and Martha soon discover that something long dormant has awoken in the town, and this will be no ordinary Halloween. What is the secret of the ancient tree and the mysterious book discovered tangled in its roots? What rises from the local churchyard in the dead of night, sealing up the lips of the only witness? And why are the harmless trappings of Halloween suddenly taking on a creepy new life of their own?

As nightmarish creatures prowl the streets, the Doctor and Martha must battle to prevent both the townspeople and themselves from suffering a grisly fate...

Wetworld

by Mark Michalowski

ISBN 978 1 84607 271 0
UK £6.99 US $11.99/$14.99 CDN

When the TARDIS makes a disastrous landing in the swamps of the planet Sunday, the Doctor has no choice but to abandon Martha and try to find help. But the tranquillity of Sunday's swamps is deceptive, and even the TARDIS can't protect Martha forever.

The human pioneers of Sunday have their own dangers to face: homeless and alone, they're only just starting to realise that Sunday's wildlife isn't as harmless as it first seems. Why are the native otters behaving so strangely, and what is the creature in the swamps that is so interested in the humans, and the new arrivals?

The Doctor and Martha must fight to ensure that human intelligence doesn't become the greatest danger of all.

DOCTOR·WHO

Creatures and Demons
by Justin Richards

ISBN 978 1 84607 229 1

UK £7.99 US $12.99/$15.99 CDN

Throughout his many adventures in time and space, the Doctor has encountered aliens, monsters, creatures and demons from right across the universe. In this third volume of alien monstrosities and dastardly villains, *Doctor Who* expert and acclaimed author Justin Richards describes some of the evils the Doctor has fought in over forty years of time travel.

From the grotesque Abzorbaloff to the monstrous Empress of the Racnoss, from giant maggots to the Daleks of the secret Cult of Skaro, from the Destroyer of Worlds to the ancient Beast itself... This book brings together more of the terrifying enemies the Doctor has battled against.

Illustrated throughout with stunning photographs and design drawings from the current series of *Doctor Who* and his previous 'classic' incarnations, this book is a treat for friends of the Doctor whatever their age, and whatever planet they come from...